Glennis, Before and After

Glennis, Before and After

Patricia Calvert

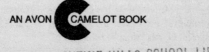

AN AVON CAMELOT BOOK

AVON BOOKS, INC.
1350 Avenue of the Americas
New York, New York 10019

First Avon Camelot Printing: January 1999

CAMELOT TRADEMARK REG. U.S. PAT. OFF. AND IN OTHER COUNTRIES, MARCA REGISTRADA,
HECHO EN U.S.A.

Printed in the U.S.A.

OPM 10 9 8 7 6 5 4 3 2

For the special ladies in my life:
Tana, Katie, Deanna,
Brianne, Dana,
and most especially, my mother, Helen Frank

❧ Chapter One

*L*ast year, after my dad was sent to prison, my mom had a nervous breakdown. *Breakdown*. That's sort of a funny word. It makes a person think of a machine that quits working, something that's got parts and pieces that need to be oiled or fixed or replaced. Well, that's pretty much how it was with my mother. Something inside her broke, and she needed to have it fixed. Anyway, that's when all us kids had to be split up and sent off to live with friends and relatives.

My brother, Vinnie—he hates the name Vincent; he says it makes him sound weird, like that famous artist who cut off part of his ear, wrapped a bandage around his head, then painted a picture of himself—went upstate to live with my grandparents.

Vinnie's the oldest, and will graduate from high school in June. There's a small college up near where Vinnie is now. I think he'll settle down and be okay. My brother just wants to forget everything that happened to him. To us. The truth is, I'm pretty sure Vinnie has always been my grandparents' favorite, so having him right there gives them plenty to do. My grandmother can keep right on believing our family isn't totally wrecked after all.

Louise went to stay with my mother's best friend, Ramona Miller, who lives back home in Kenwood and teaches fifth grade at Gibson Middle School. Ramona and her husband, Robert, never had any kids. They tried to adopt one once, but the agency came back with the bad news they were too old.

"How can you be too old to love a child?" Ramona asked, and cried in my mother's arms as if suddenly she were a brokenhearted, homeless child herself. Naturally, Ramona and Robert were thrilled to get someone really nice like my sister Louise, even though it might only be temporary and she's practically grown-up besides. You want to know something else? I think Louise was thrilled to get them, too.

"They treat me like a princess," she said in the first letter she wrote after we all got split up. She's the only one in the family who wrote to me regularly. "Before, I was famous mostly for being born two years after Vinnie." I was surprised; except for being a few pounds overweight (my mother told Louise not to worry, it was only baby fat), I always thought my sister seemed pretty pleased with herself.

Allyssa and Melyssa (Allie and Missy to everyone who knows them) are only six, and got shipped off to my uncle Roger. He's got two kids of his own, big, noisy jocks in junior high who do every sport known to a rec director, which is exactly what my uncle Roger is. Basketball, football, hockey, baseball—you name it, my cousins Derek and Jason slam-dunk it, pass it, or hit it with a stick. So Roger and my aunt Helen didn't mind getting a pair of twin girls with blue eyes and wavy yellow hair whose idea of a wild time is coloring outside the lines in their first-grade workbooks.

Rags, the gold-and-white collie we got Christmas Eve the year I was seven, had to be given to the Mumfords down the road. It might sound funny, but for me to know Rags would be somebody else's dog was the worst part of all. I cried till I thought I'd never quit the night the Mumfords drove off with him in their station wagon.

Me?

I'm Glennis, and I've heard enough stupid "How about a game of tennis, Glennis?" cracks to last me till I'm ninety.

Right now, though, I'm at that peculiar no-age age. Older than twelve, not quite thirteen yet. Too old to be treated as tenderly as the twins, not old enough to be taken super-seriously like Vinnie or Louise. Also, I am your basic, generic Invisible Person. Not because people don't like me—actually, I think most people like me pretty well, mainly because I don't make trouble or demand attention.

At school, girls have never been jealous of my long, blond, naturally curly hair, because it's short, brown, and straight. Boys never give me a hard time, because (a) I'm not too smart, but (b) I'm not too dumb. Teachers usually are crazy about me because I have this wonderful talent. I'm cooperative. Listen, you want a kid who's easy to get along with? A kid who follows orders, never makes waves, gets her homework done on time? Step right up, folks; Glennis Reilly's the girl for you.

I got sent to my mother's sister, Wanda, who—up till my dad went to prison—was the only black sheep in our family. Relatives on both sides always said my mother was lucky to have married so well, but that poor Wanda just got married. And married. And married.

"I guess she's still trying to get it right," I overheard Uncle Roger tell my dad once. My mother, her sister, Wanda, and their brother, Roger, came from what some people call the wrong side of the tracks, though you'd never have known it to look at my mother. After my parents were married, Mom said my grandmother Reilly taught her how to dress the right way. The way my mom said it made me think she had other ideas, that maybe she might have liked clothes that were more like a gypsy's, but was too scared of my grandmother to go against her wishes.

"Pale, neutral colors are always more tasteful," my grandmother advised, and never bought Louise or me stuff that was too loud or bright, either. Her favorite shade was something called taupe, which is sort of gray- ish beige with a hint of lavender thrown in. My aunt Wanda, on the other hand, favors black jeans, purple shirts with colored rhinestones, and cowboy boots decor- ated with designs of lariats and cactuses. Some people would call her a character; to me, she was just Aunt Wanda.

Lucky for me, Wanda is currently unattached. She has one son, my cousin Skipper, who's in second grade, sniffles a lot, and has an undernourished, poster child look about him.

Don't get the wrong idea, though. I didn't get stuck with Wanda and Skipper because anybody forced me to go live with them, even though I'm the middle kid and sometimes get taken for granted.

The reason I got Wanda is because I asked for her.

At first, the whole family was shocked.

"Out of the question," my grandmother declared. She

crossed her arms, and narrowed her eyes like a general plotting important new strategies on a battlefield. Her snowy hair swept back from each side of her brow like silver wings, and her profile was as clean and sharp as one on a brand-new coin as we discussed the matter in her living room after my mother broke down.

One thing about my grandmother: She definitely came from the right side of the tracks, and there's plenty about her to remind even strangers of that fact. We kids didn't forget it, either, because she wanted all of us to call her Nana. She didn't like the sound of the name *Grandma.* She said she wasn't your grandma type of person, the kind who smiles a lot, bakes brownies, and wears an apron.

"Wanda can barely take care of her own child, let alone anyone else's," Nana informed me, leaving no doubt that she considered Wanda to be the perfect example of a nightmare mom from hell.

My grandfather listened, and drummed a careful tattoo on his knee. He adjusted his glasses, then nodded in agreement. Not necessarily because he agreed with Nana, but he knew from experience it was pretty hard to argue with her.

Later, Vinnie and Louise took me aside. "Are you sure this is where you want to go?" my brother asked. He looked at me as if he were seeing me for the first time in a long while. His brown eyes were filled with worry, an unusual expression for Vinnie.

"Definitely," I said, which relieved him so much the worry vanished from his eyes in a flash, making me wonder if I'd seen it there in the first place.

Louise held both of my hands in hers. "Listen, sweetie, you don't have to make a sacrificial lamb out of yourself," she pointed out. Her voice was soft and mild, which pretty much describes what my sister looks like all over. Unlike our grandmother, Louise is a person without any sharp edges or angles. She moves through rooms, down hallways, or across lawns like a girl floating along in a dream.

"I didn't put in a request for Wanda because she's a sheep or because I'm a lamb," I said, and took my hands back. Not because Wanda let it be known she needed a baby-sitter for Skipper, either. She did, but I didn't know anything about that till I went to live with her.

I asked for Wanda because she lived in Burnsville, down in the southeastern corner of the state along the Union River, which is famous in Ohio mostly for one thing. It's where the prison is.

That's where I wanted to be.

Okay, so my dad got put away (I hate the sound of those words, *put away*). Okay, so it's true he'll be in prison a good long while. But deep inside, where nobody knows I go to hide as if it were a cellar I could crawl into and pull a door shut after me, I knew my dad didn't do all that stuff everyone said he did at the trial. My dad never said he was guilty. If he had been, he would've admitted it. He wouldn't lie. Not my dad.

I couldn't go to prison with him or for him, but for sure I could stick as close as I could. I wanted to be one of the reasons my father stayed connected to the world he had to leave behind. When he got out, there I'd be—Glennis, the one in the family who'd always loved him best before and would still love him best after. The kid in the middle, the one hardly anyone ever paid much attention to. The one who knew someday, some way we'd all be a real family again.

It just killed me to think how it was for my dad there

at the end. He probably felt cut off from everyone he loved. As if he were a man adrift on an ice floe way up there in the Arctic, a man who couldn't do anything to keep the distance between himself and the rest of us from growing wider and wider, until finally we couldn't make ourselves heard across the dark, frozen space that separated us.

Because of what the prosecution lawyers said he'd done, our family had changed completely. Like Humpty Dumpty, someone shoved us off a high wall, and we'd been broken into a kazillion million pieces. If a person listed the biggest ones, it got positively scary.

Dad was in prison.

Mom was having a breakdown.

Vinnie wanted to forget he was related to any of us.

Louise felt special for the first time in her life.

Allie and Missy were being raised right beside two lunky, clunky jocks with brains the size of prune pits.

I was living with someone who wore rhinestone cowboy shirts.

Rags was some other family's favorite pooch.

Listen. I just couldn't stand to think of my dad carrying that load all by himself. Which is the reason I asked for Wanda.

To my surprise, I got her. Got my cousin Skipper, too. Got the prison at the edge of town, a new school, a tacky room in Wanda's upstairs that she'd used for years to store broken-down furniture and boxes of scraps she's saving to make into a quilt someday.

I also got something I never counted on. I found out webs aren't only for spiders. And not all prisons are made out of stone.

🌸 Chapter Two

After I went to live at Wanda's, Saturday was my favorite day of the week even more than it'd been before. For starters, it was the only time I had the kitchen all to myself. Well, almost. Sugar, Aunt Wanda's old cat, was usually waiting for me, hoping to get an early bowl of milk warmed up in the microwave.

Sugar was just about the same vanilla color as the Irish cable-knit sweater I wore every Saturday. Mom bought it in Dublin when she and Dad went there on vacation once. That was right after Allie and Missy were born, and my parents called it their second honeymoon. They hired a lady to come in and take care of the rest of us, and we sort of felt like we were on vacation, too.

Now that she's busy having a breakdown, though, most days my mother doesn't care what she wears or even if she combs her hair or brushes her teeth. That's why I packed her sweater with my stuff when I left home. The doctor said the new pills my mother's taking will help her get better quicker. When she does, I'll give the sweater back. But wearing it makes me feel close to her. Like she's got her arms around me, as if she's not in that place called Fair Haven.

Mainly, though, Saturday was my favorite day because that's when I went out to the prison. A person my age was supposed to go with someone older, so my grandmother had to write her congressman for special permission so I could by myself.

"Glennis's mother is seriously ill," Nana explained. "Her aunt, with whom she is now residing, has too many other responsibilities, and I myself live at the opposite end of the state, making it impossible for me to accompany Glennis on weekly visits to see her father. Therefore, I need your help in placing my granddaughter's name on the list of approved visitors at the prison." My grandmother reminded Mr. Willis she was one of his faithful campaign contributors, and got a nice letter right back saying he'd be happy to take care of her request.

After I warmed Sugar's milk, I got an apple out of the fridge, washed it, and dried it on a paper towel. It was for eating later, on the bus. Then I made myself some cocoa and cinnamon toast. I'd been doing exactly the same thing every weekend since I came to Burnsville.

By the time I finished my breakfast, Sugar was done with hers, too. She sat beside her calico basket in the corner of the kitchen and cleaned her silver whiskers, her yellow eyes closed with contentment.

"So long, Sugar-Baby," I whispered, and headed for the back door. I hung on to it as I went out, because it was blowing hard from the northeast, and I knew its rusty hinges would squeak like crazy if the wind caught it.

9

Wanda often had to work the night shift on Friday at the Sup-R-Chef downtown, and liked things to be quiet so she could sleep in late on Saturday. When Skipper finally got up, I knew he'd turn cartoons on real low, and get himself a bowl of Tootie Frooties to eat in front of the TV. I closed the door; it was another safe, no-squeak morning.

In my former life (that's how I thought of it now), Saturday was for mall ratting. I'd usually meet Dee and Renae at the Village Square, then we'd schmooze around. Meet a few other kids around noon. Eat giant hot pretzels from the kiosk near the Shirt Shed store. Those days passed so quickly, the next thing I knew it was time for church on Sunday.

Today the wind coming off the Union River beyond the railroad tracks was cold, and I hunched inside my jacket. Wanda's neighborhood was the bleak, run-down kind, where all the houses needed paint, the sidewalks had gotten crumbly, and hardly anyone planted flowers anymore. I saw the bus round the corner a block away. Sheesh! Somehow I'd gotten behind schedule. I sprinted hard for the next corner. No time to dream about how life was before; this was after.

The usual bunch was already on the bus, all of them headed for the prison just like me. The driver was new, though.

I was disappointed; I liked the old one better. Because he *was* old, and looked like somebody's granddad. My own, even. You know, the kind with silver hair and twinkly blue eyes nestled in pockets of crepe-paper flesh. A Santa Claus type of guy, with an honest face.

An honest face.

Better leave that one alone, Glennis, I told myself.

The old codger might be keeping as many secrets as people said Dad and the guys in his office had.

After the trial, I came to one conclusion. You can't always tell from the outside of a person what the inside's really like. Look at Mr. Endersen, as pale and pious as a saint, but what a mess he dragged my dad into. A mess that broke my family into those jagged pieces I'd spend the rest of my life gluing back together again.

I dumped a dollar's worth of tokens into the coin box, then grabbed the handrail and headed down the aisle toward the back. I avoided everyone's glance as carefully as they avoided mine. I plopped down, and waited for the best part of the trip.

Going out and coming back from the prison, I usually got a glimpse of the swans in the city park. Back home, I'd been able to see swans on the pond the Mumfords had in their backyard about a quarter of a mile away. Seeing swans every Saturday in Burnsville made me feel practically normal.

It was cold, and only a small, dark, oval patch of water was still unfrozen for the birds to paddle around in. A week ago, I'd seen them waddle across the ice at the edge of the pond to be fed by a groundskeeper who waited with a plastic bucket filled with lettuce and bread. I spotted some nesting boxes in the frozen reeds, too. In another month when all the ice was melted, would these swans have babies swimming behind them like pull-toys on a string, like the birds on the Mumfords' pond did every spring?

When we passed the park, there was no groundskeeper anywhere. The birds weren't swimming, either. I figured they must be huddled inside the shelter that had been built for them nearby. I polished my apple on my sleeve, and settled down to my other Saturday hobby—looking at the backs of the heads of the other passengers. I passed the time by thinking up names and histories for them.

Mrs. Cinnamon Buns sat three seats in front of me. The whole bus was fragrant with the homemade goodies she balanced on her knees in a square white box. I decided she was probably taking them out to her only son, a college kid who'd been a straight-A student. He'd planned to be a doctor till he got in with the wrong crowd and started dealing drugs to his buddies.

A couple seats in front of her was the Movie Star. Her hair was the color of saltwater taffy but dark at the roots. Her fingernails were the gruesome shade of a dragon's blood, and she always wore dark glasses. Her career had gone into a tailspin after her boyfriend was sent to prison, but now her agent was trying to get a new deal for her in Hollywood.

The Godfather sat across the aisle. I named him the Godfather because he wore a fawn-colored coat and beautiful matching gloves, like a guy did in a Mafia movie I saw once on late-night TV when I was baby-sitting Allie and Missy. I figured he went out once a week to visit Dirty Dog O'Donovan, one of his old cronies from the mob.

I blinked. I blinked again.

There was a new person on the bus.

Which would've been enough of a surprise. I mean, having seen the same bunch of people for almost three months, I wasn't exactly expecting anyone new. The other part of the surprise was that he was around my brother Vinnie's age. For some weird reason he looked almost familiar. Why should he? I mean, I'd never seen him before.

I'd named everyone else on the bus, had invented lives for them, so what should this new guy be called? What kind of history should I give him?

He turned to stare out the window of the bus. His nose was smooshed into his face, sort of like a prize-fighter's. He looked sour, and frowned in a crabby way at his reflection in the dusty green glass.

I was about to pull a name out of the air (I leaned toward Rocky, and decided maybe he was training for a lightweight match in New Jersey) when I heard the air brakes squeal. Beyond the bus window a yellow sign with black letters slid under my nose.

FEDERAL DETENTION CENTER. No matter how often I saw it, that sign always surprised me.

It was still hard to believe that's where my dad lived now. Not by day in a nice office on the tenth floor of the Sterling Savings and Loan, where the carpet was thick and the furniture was dark. Not by night in a tall white house set on two acres of green lawn, with a wife and five kids, including me.

He was in prison now. Not just any old prison, either, but one for men who were guilty of federal crimes. Those are the kind committed against the whole country and its laws, not just against individual people. You know—bank fraud, illegal stock market trading, spying for foreign countries, kidnapping, killing a police officer—heavy-duty stuff like that. During the trial, the media always referred to what my dad did as a white-collar crime, to set it apart from what most people think of as the real kind committed by guys who don't shave every day and never wear suits or ties.

My father was a convict now. Which made me a convict's daughter. He wouldn't be eligible for a parole hearing for at least three years. Neither would I. And if he had to serve his whole ten-year sentence, I'd be almost twenty-three years old by the time he got out. My hair might have turned gray from the strain of the faithful vigil I'd kept.

The stranger—I didn't have time to settle on a name or a history for him—was off the bus the second it pulled up in front of the prison doors, then he vanished into thin air. Since I was at the back of the bus, I was the last to get off. I passed the seat where Mr. Mysterious had been sitting. Lying there was a small green notebook. The cheap kind a person would buy to keep people's names and phone numbers in if he didn't want to spend big bucks on a real address book.

I wondered if I ought to give it to the bus driver. If the old guy had been driving, that's exactly what I would've done. But there was something off-putting about this new one, who didn't smile at any of us or say something nice, like, "Good morning" or, "See you later."

I picked up the notebook and stuck it in my jacket pocket. I would return it to its owner next week. I promised myself I wouldn't open it or read anything that was inside.

I lied, though.

Maybe that came as easy to me as everyone said it did to my dad.

🌺 *Chapter Three*

*L*et's face it: Dad wasn't exactly thrilled the first time I visited him.

I suppose he was embarrassed. He kept his eyes fastened on his knuckles as if there were an important message tattooed on each one. So I tried to look at it from his point of view.

Once, he'd been somebody special, not just because he was our dad, but because he really was. The den back home was filled with photographs of him at all stages of his life. With his parents when they were young, and didn't look anything like the white-haired people we kids knew. He was their only child, which probably was one of the reasons he felt so special right from the beginning. His being the only son was why my grandparents—especially my grandmother—were so glad to get their hands on Vinnie after the trial.

There were pictures of Dad in baseball caps and football helmets. In tennis shorts and skiing gear. In his Annapolis uniform. Getting married. Holding each of us kids at our baptisms. In those pictures, he was always smiling. My mother looked happy, a tall, slim woman whose eyes glowed like two dark stars in her narrow face. In the background, the sun always seemed to be shining; there were never any clouds.

"So how'd school go this week, Glennis?" he asked as soon as I sat next to him in the visitor's lounge. Now that I've visited him every Saturday for almost three months, he seems to look forward to seeing me, and always asks the same question. Never once has he ever called me Glennie, though, or made any stupid tennis cracks.

I nodded. "Pretty good. I'm getting used to everyone. They're getting used to me. You know how it is when you have to start in a new school. It just takes time."

The truth was, I was still a stranger at Edison Middle School. Most people hate that feeling, and knock themselves out trying to make friends and get into a group. I didn't. I was still a stranger because that's exactly what I wanted to be.

It was Dad's turn to nod. "You finally getting into some activities?" he wanted to know. "Back in Kenwood you were in choir, remember? I always liked going to your school concerts, Glennis. And how about that swim meet in fifth grade when you got second place? Your mother had your ribbon framed, remember? She hung it in the upstairs hall along with all Vinnie's awards." His voice took on a thin, faraway sound.

Remember? Sure I did. But I didn't have a clue about whatever happened to my framed ribbon or to all of Vinnie's stuff. When the trial was over, our big white house had to be sold. Everything that we loved was packed up—lamps, books, furniture, the paintings on the walls—and moved upstate to a huge storage shed on the back of my grandparents' big place near the lake. In that house, Vinnie was living in my dad's old room now. Using my dad's old desk. Sleeping in my dad's old bed. Letting my grandmother turn him into a reflection of the boy who'd lived there first. And if I knew Vinnie like I thought I knew him, he was probably a happy camper.

"Mostly, I'm too busy for choir or swimming," I told Dad. "Anyway, there's Skipper. Wanda never asks me to baby-sit or anything like that," I added quickly, "but I don't mind doing it."

I didn't want my dad to get the idea that Wanda was leaning on me even a teeny-weeny bit. If he did, he might write a letter to Nana, who'd probably make me leave Burnsville. "For your own good," she'd tell me, which was her favorite reason for deciding a lot of things.

Soon, our conversation developed a hump in the middle. It usually did after we'd visited for about ten or fifteen minutes.

"Skipper watches too much TV," I said, just to have something else to talk about, but it was true. Around us, other prisoners gossiped with their visitors, and I looked around for Mr. Mysterious. I fingered the notebook in my pocket, but didn't see him anywhere.

"My English teacher, Mrs. McCarthy, quit smoking two weeks ago," I went on, as if Dad were interested, which I knew he probably wasn't. "She says her nerves feel as if somebody sandpapered them till they're like raw hamburger."

Dad gave me a one-sided smile. "That's a tough one, all right," he agreed. "Tell her for me it's worth it, so she just better hang in there."

No way did I intend to tell Mrs. McCarthy any such thing.

She might ask me for details about him. Where he worked; if a job transfer was the reason we'd moved to Burnsville; if I had any brothers and sisters. Nobody at school knew much about me, and for sure I planned to keep it that way. If anyone asked personal questions, I delivered this well-rehearsed little speech I'd made up.

"I came to live with my aunt Wanda and my cousin Skipper because of, ah, um, certain family problems." I made the confession softly, lowered my eyes, and chewed on my lip. I knew exactly how people translated remarks like that, because I'd done it a few times myself: "Wow. Too bad. Sounds like her folks are getting a divorce."

They weren't—not yet, anyway—but it was easier than telling the truth. I mean, how would it sound?

"Listen up, you guys, here's the official scoop. One, my dad's in the detention center, a fact that, two, unhinged my mother so bad that, three, she had to go to Fair Haven to get over a breakdown, the result of which was, four, my brother and sister and the twins and I got passed around to friends and relatives like cookies on a plate."

Please. Anyway, how could I ever make anyone understand that once upon a time heaven was a place where I'd actually lived? In a house on a hill, with wonderful parents, a brother, three sisters, and a dog named Rags? How could I ever explain to strangers that my whole family had drifted so far apart it would take a miracle for all of us to find our way back together again? Forget it. A made-up story was easier.

The hump grew bigger between Dad and me, and it wasn't long before one of those flat, toneless voices announced over the intercom that visiting hours were over. It said the bus would be loading out front in a few minutes.

"Glennis, there's something I've been wanting to tell you," Dad blurted out when I got up to leave. His voice was urgent and strained. There was an unused, rusty sound in it that made me think of the hinges on Wanda's back door.

When I looked up at him I realized he was about to lay some really important news on me. His lips were parted; the words struggled with each other to shove their way past his teeth. His eyes are dark brown, just like Vinnie's, and they suddenly became a pair of bottomless wells. I felt as if I were being lowered slowly down, down into them.

He's finally going to tell me, I thought, and my heart went absolutely still in my chest, like a rabbit huddled under a bush. I waited, not breathing, for what he'd say next.

My dream was going to come true! Finally, Dad would fill me in on the plan he had for getting a new trial. He would give me instructions about how I could help him. I might have to write a letter to the governor. The president, even. It was the reason I'd come to Burnsville, just to hear what he was going to tell me. The Reillys' nightmare would soon be over. Everything we had before would come back to us. We'd all be happy again.

Instead, my dad swallowed hard, pushed the words back where they'd come from, and muttered, "Listen, Bunny, thanks for coming out here every Saturday. It means more to me than I can ever tell you."

It wasn't what I'd been waiting to hear, but the name he used made my heart start to thonk again. *Bunny.* It was a nickname from that faraway time when we were still a family. "Before everything fell apart," to use Dad's phrase from when the scandal was at its height. When his face was in all the newspapers, not to mention on TV every night. It was a soft, fuzzy name, a security blanket name. I wasn't a security blanket kind of kid anymore, but I'd always loved how that name sounded whenever he said it.

"See you next week," I promised, disappointed that he wasn't ready yet to give me any instructions about a new trial. Then I decided maybe he still had to think through some important details. But next week—for sure, next week—he'd tell me about his plans.

I prayed silently that he wouldn't wait too much longer, because after I moved in with Wanda I sat down and counted up ten years' worth of Saturday mornings. Came to about 520. They stretched endlessly before me, as long and lonesome as the Oregon Trail. I felt like an orphan pioneer child, trailing West behind all the people who belonged to each other, while I had to make the trip across the prairie all by myself. Okay, so I wasn't really an orphan, but that's exactly how I felt a lot of the time.

Everyone got back on the bus, everyone, that is, except Mr. Mysterious. I switched seats for the trip back, so I'd be on the side facing the park and would get a second chance to see the swans. I stuffed my hands in my jacket pocket, and ran my thumb down the spiral backbone of the notebook.

Sure enough, the swans were out. Lemon-colored March sunshine made the dark oval in the ice look blacker than ever. The groundskeeper had arrived with a bucket of bread and lettuce. The swans lumbered toward him, as clumsy on land as they were graceful in the water.

The keeper threw out pieces of lettuce and bread, and as the bus rolled by, I glimpsed his profile. His nose was smooshed into his face like a prizefighter's. His expression was sour. He caught sight of me peering out the bus window at the same instant I saw him. He lifted his hand and waved.

I rode for a whole block, hardly breathing, before I took the notebook out of my pocket.

There wasn't any name on the outside. If I opened it, I knew I'd be prying into the affairs of a total stranger. After another block, that's what I gave myself permission to do.

On the first page a name was printed in careful letters: Cooper Davis. There was a peculiar address: c/o PORT, 124 Ash Street, Burnsville, OH. I was pretty sure there weren't any ports in Burnsville. The Union River was way too shallow for any sort of barge traffic. I turned the page. On it was a poem.

Pigeons and Prisoners, I read, surprised.

Cooper Davis—whose nose was flattened into his face like a thug's, who was about the same age as my brother, Vinnie, who looked like a guy getting ready for a comeback lightweight match in New Jersey—wrote *poetry?* Silently, I mouthed the words in front of me.

> *The pigeons on the courthouse lintel*
> *Were beige and blue and brown.*
> *Only one was white. They were beautiful;*
> *Birds usually are.*
> *And while the guilty claim their innocence,*
> *Others declare it's as fixed*
> *As a stone, a leaf, a star.*

21

I snapped the book shut. Its cover felt uncommonly warm and smooth under my fingertips. Something weird had just happened, but it took me a minute to figure out what it was. The cellar door deep down inside, where I often went to hide in the dark, had opened a crack.

No way could I talk to Mrs. McCarthy or anyone else at school about why I'd come to live with Wanda and Skipper. Or that I was sure my dad was innocent of the crime everybody said he committed. Or that I believed if I worked hard enough and waited long enough, I'd be able to glue my family back together again.

But Cooper Davis, who was about the same age as Vinnie, must know a prisoner at the Federal Detention Center, just like I did. A brother? A father, like mine? I wouldn't need to explain anything to Cooper Davis. He already knew stuff about guilt and innocence. Not to mention something about stones and leaves and stars.

Cooper Davis would be someone I could talk to.

🌹 *Chapter Four*

*T*here was a note in the middle of the kitchen table when I got back to Wanda's.

> *Be a good kid, Glen, and fix some lunch for Skipper, okay? Angie got sick again, so I had to report for the second shift. Thankx, W.*

I crumpled the note into a ball. Wanda turned *s*'s into *x*'s, and now I was a Glen.

I could hear the TV going—loud now, because Skipper knew his mom wasn't sleeping anymore. His eyeballs were attached to the screen by two invisible wires. The only time they moved was to follow some cartoon character's flight over a cliff or down some rat-filled sewer. I reached over and switched the set off.

Skipper let out a yowl. "Turn that back on!" he squawked. "The Road Runner was just about to get—"

"Sure. Tell me about it. Flattened, smashed, stretched, shot, and drowned—all at the same time, right?'' He glared at me, his face pinched and outraged. ''You watch too many violent cartoons, Skipper. You're ruining your eyes, not to mention your delicate mental health.''

''What d'you care about my eyes or my mental health?'' he screeched, and reached for the On button.

''Touch that, chum, and you're toast,'' I warned. ''C'mon, I'll fix us something to eat.'' It was way past noon; he probably was as starved as I was myself.

One thing about Skipper: His outrages don't last long. He dragged himself listlessly after me into the kitchen. He'd watched the tube till he was exhausted, hadn't exercised anything all morning except those bloodshot eyeballs. The kid was destined to wither away, become a weak old man even before he was one.

I opened Wanda's cupboards. At home, ours were full of stuff like cans of green beans and peaches and pears. We had a freezer with lots of other stuff in it—beef and chicken and fish. Here, dozens and dozens of boxes stared me in the face. I exaggerate—but not much. I'd lived at Wanda's for three months, and every night we had something that came out of a box. Mostly something with cheese in it. No wonder Skipper had such a pasty complexion, with a strong tinge of cheddar to it.

I clapped the cupboard doors shut. ''I'll cook us up something from scratch,'' I told him.

''From scratch? What's that mean? I bet I won't like it,'' he grumbled. He sat at the table with his chin in his hands, as worn out as if he'd been digging ditches since sunup.

I scrambled some eggs and warmed up a couple muffins from two nights ago. I found a jar of applesauce and opened it. There were a few lonesome carrots in the veggie keeper; I scraped them and cut them into sticks.

"That looks like a carrot," Skipper accused, his eyes squinty with suspicion.

"It is. Try one," I invited. "They're good for you." Poor little guy; it was plain he'd never eaten a carrot stick before.

He bit into one, then scowled. "This stuff is noisy," he complained.

"Compared to macaroni and cheese, practically any food would be noisy," I pointed out.

After we ate, I cleaned up the dishes, wiped the table off, then asked Skipper if he wanted to go for a walk.

"A walk?" he echoed, astonished. He'd handled the carrot stick crisis okay, so I figured he could handle this challenge, too. "You mean, just go out there and . . . *walk?*"

It probably was the first time he'd done anything like that for pure pleasure. Back home, my whole family walked the length of Stone Barn Road after supper a couple evenings each week. We held hands (not Vinnie, of course, who thought he was way too old for hand-holding) while we watched the sun go down behind the hill. My dad used to say that it was the perfect way to unwind after a hard day at the office.

"Maybe a walk will put a little color in your cheeks," I told Skipper. It was exactly the kind of uplifting, for-your-own-good remark my grandmother would make.

The wind had died off, and the chill from the river wasn't as bad as it'd been earlier in the day. Last summer's dried weeds stood as high as my head next to the abandoned boxcars across the street, and rustled lightly in the breeze that was left. Down the block, somebody's dog barked; I tried not to think about Rags.

"So how much longer are you going to stay with me and Mom?" Skipper wanted to know.

"You're tired of me already?" I sighed. Not good news—especially considering I might be around for ten whole years. "You planning to rent out those first-class accommodations upstairs to someone who can pay more rent, or what?"

"I like you okay." Skipper got quiet, and seemed to be thinking hard. "It's sort of nice having someone around. You know, like a sister or something."

"I'm definitely in the 'or something' category, all right," I agreed.

Skipper was silent for another half a block. "What's it like out there?" he asked finally.

"Out where?"

"At the prison."

"Nicer than you might think," I said, surprised he was curious. I was glad he'd asked, though, because I realized I wanted to talk about it myself. "It's not like on TV. The detention center isn't one of those maximum-security prisons, so I don't have to visit my dad through a thick sheet of glass or a wire screen or anything like that. We sit in the visitors' lounge. Actually, it's sort of like a big living room, with couches and chairs and stuff. They've got machines for Coke and other ones where you can buy candy bars or cookies. Lots of other people are there, too, visiting with their relatives. Some play cards or watch TV."

"I sure hope I don't grow up to be a convict," Skipper said. There was a spooked tone in his voice, so I knew he'd been thinking for a while about the possibility he might.

"Most people don't plan to grow up and go to prison," I told him. For sure my dad hadn't.

"But it could happen," Skipper insisted. "It sure did to your daddy."

Ouch! Out of the mouths of babes, like it says in Psalms. Yes, it had happened to my dad, a fact I still couldn't explain to myself, much less to Skipper. Except that I knew somehow my dad had gotten trapped.

"Sometimes things just happen, Skipper," I said. I knew in my heart my dad was taking the punishment for someone else. Maybe he was even being blackmailed by evil Mr. Endersen, who was still walking around looking saintly but had a heart as black as coal. Mr. Endersen might have hired someone to threaten my dad.

"Keep your mouth shut, John Reilly," a tall guy with hooded eyes and a black mustache would have warned him. The man with him would be short and covered with tattoos; they might have followed Dad into that new parking ramp next to his office. They might've waved a gun in his face, or held a knife against his ribs. "If you don't, we'll make sure you never see your wife and kids alive again."

I knew my dad would've done anything in the world to keep us all safe. In fact, the more I thought about it, the surer I was that it had been a threat of harm to us that had kept him silent this morning, had made him swallow whatever he'd almost been ready to tell me.

"I've got this theory, Skipper," I explained. "You can trust your best friends, and think everything's fine. You don't realize things are creeping up on you so slow and quiet that you haven't even noticed. Then all of a sudden you're in a courtroom, and someone from a jury says, 'Guilty as charged on all counts.' Right then, you realize nothing was like you always thought it was."

When a verdict like that was read out loud, probably no one was more surprised than you were yourself. So in a way, maybe Skipper wasn't so crazy to be worried.

It could happen to anyone—to him, to me—just like it'd happened to my dad.

In the life we had before, Dad was vice president of the Sterling Savings and Loan. *Sterling.* That name was so solid; people used it in common phrases that nobody thinks much about at the time, like, "He has a sterling character," or, "That company is as solid as a pound of sterling."

Yet the newspapers said Dad had robbed old people, widows, and orphans of their security. One picture in the *Kenwood Times* showed an old woman in front of the SS&L on the morning the federal officers came from Washington, D.C., to lock the doors and seal them with huge strips of yellow tape that said, CRIME SCENE. NO TRESPASSING. She had a scarf tied under her chin, and dabbed at her eyes with a handkerchief. A man with a TV camera interviewed her, and she said she'd lost everything she owned.

"I don't know what will happen to me now," she said, her chin quivering, tears making silver tracks down her cheeks. But I knew my dad would never do anything to hurt a person like her, any more than he'd steal from my grandmother.

Skipper and I went up to the playground at Edison, where we played on the swings for a while. During the day, kids Skipper's age were at one end of the building in the elementary section, while kids my age were at the opposite end in middle school. Only there's nothing lonesomer when the sun begins to go down than an empty playground, so finally we left.

We walked around for a long time before we headed back home. That's when Skipper told me, in a dreamy voice filled with wishes, that he'd almost joined peewee wrestling at the beginning for the year.

"Almost? So how come you didn't?" I asked.

"Because those big kids would probably kill me," he said.

"They don't make you wrestle any big kids, Skipper, and I bet nobody ever got murdered in peewee wrestling," I told him. I knew exactly how those matches were arranged, how kids were paired with someone their own size and age and weight, because Vinnie wrestled from the time he was even littler than Skipper. "Maybe you should reconsider and give it a try."

"I'm not crazy!" Skipper declared. "Stuff like that's not for kids like me." I wondered what kind of a kid he thought he was. When we got closer to home, I noticed the scarlet sky had stained the fronts of the tacky old houses on Wanda's street the color of cranberry juice. The hard edges of the railroad cars were softened in the falling light, and the weeds around them looked like feathery jungle ferns.

Skipper reached for my hand and changed the subject. "That stuff you made from scratch was okay," he admitted in a shy voice. His fingers were sticky against mine. "You got any scratch ideas for supper, Glennis?"

Oh! Such a queer, mournful feeling filled me up that my throat clamped shut and I couldn't answer him right away. We think we know the people we live with, what they feel, what their lives are like. Maybe we never do, though.

Till today I'd never really thought about the fact Skipper never ate much that didn't come out of a cardboard box. I've been in his house for three months and never noticed the little guy didn't even know what a carrot stick was. He'd lived an add-water-and-mix kind of life, which was news to me even though he was my very own cousin and I'd seen him every Christmas and usually at the family picnics we had in our backyard on Memorial Day.

And nobody knew—not my brother or sisters or mother or grandparents—that I believed Dad was innocent. Or that I dreamed someday I'd be able to help him prove it. Nobody knew about that dream because no one ever asked. And I never told.

❧ Chapter Five

*T*he notebook was in my pocket, ready to be handed over to its owner. When I got on the bus the next Saturday, I scanned the passengers as I walked down the aisle toward the back.

My plan was simple: I'd hold the notebook out, Cooper Davis would take it, then he'd scoot over so I could sit down beside him. But the seat he'd been in the week before was empty. When we passed the swans, though, there he was, out early with his bucket of bread and lettuce. I was disappointed. There was a lot of stuff I wanted to talk to him about.

Then, when I got to the FDC, Dad didn't seem as glad to see me as he'd been lately. Something seemed to be bugging him more than usual.

I wasn't surprised. For me to get used to a new school or to Wanda's junk-filled upstairs bedroom was probably a picnic compared to what he had to go through every single day at the FDC. For starters, he woke up every morning to see bars on his window, and had to eat breakfast at a long, metal table with a dozen other guys dressed in orange coveralls exactly like his. Instead of giving orders, now he had to follow ones somebody gave him.

"You started to tell me something last week," I reminded him as soon as we got settled. "The intercom interrupted you, remember?"

He gave me a glazed look, and massaged his forehead with all ten fingers. "Bunny, no matter what you think, it really would be better if you hadn't come to live in Burnsville. It was a terrible mistake for Nana to allow you to stay with Wanda. Not that Wanda's a bad person or anything like that," he added quickly. "She's your mother's sister, after all, and she's got a heart of gold, but I think you should have—"

"Oh, Wanda's not leaning on me even a teeny-weeny bit," I explained, exactly as I had the week before. "The only reason I help out with Skipper sometimes is because I want to. He says it's nice to have someone around who's like a sister." Dad didn't look up at me.

"Anyway, if I wasn't living with Wanda, how could I visit you once a week? I want to be here so I can help you as soon as you figure out a way to get a new trial." I knew he couldn't tell me his plans yet, but I figured it would relieve his mind if he knew I was ready to help the minute he was.

"New trial?" he echoed.

"It's okay, Dad. You don't have to talk about it until you've got all the details figured out. Afterward, we can get our old life back. Our old house, Rags, everything. Till then, just remember, I'm here. I'll do whatever you need me to do." It felt good to get the words right out.

"But, Glennis—" He interrupted himself, a dead sound in his voice. I noticed he wasn't using my old security-blanket name anymore. "It's not good for you to plan your life around me, Glennis. Coming out here every Saturday shouldn't be part of a weekly routine for any girl your age." Finally, he glanced up. His mouth smiled; his eyes didn't.

"They've got a saying in here," he went on slowly, and tried to make his fingers stay still on the table between us. "You do the crime, you do the time. That's what men here say, Glennis, and they're one hundred percent on target. You didn't do any crime, sweetheart, and there's no way you can do my time, either."

"It's okay, Dad. Really," I assured him. I considered reminding him that I was almost thirteen. "School's getting a lot better," I said instead. "There's this bunch of girls who are beginning to like me a little, and Wanda said maybe she'll paint that room upstairs for me." Right now it was covered with old stuff printed with faded yellow roses, paper whose dried-out seams curled outward like zippers that didn't zip anymore.

"I really wish you'd gone with Louise to stay at Ramona's," Dad insisted. His voice still had a funny dead sound in it. He pressed his thumbs against his temples, making a visor out of the other eight fingers so he could shade his eyes from mine. If I'd gone to Ramona's, Louise wouldn't be enjoying herself right now as a princess. Anyway, no one asked me to go to there, but I didn't want to point that fact out to him.

I got a checkerboard off the game shelf in the visitors' room and we played. Just as well, because neither of us had much more to say. He made a ton of mistakes and I wiped him out. He hugged me lightly when it was time for me to go (he felt thin under his orange coveralls, and his backbone was knobby), then I was outside again. The bus was loading. The grandfather driver was back on duty, and he beckoned to me with a smile. "Climb on board, girlie," he said.

I waved him on. I'd decided to walk back to town. It was only about two miles or so, and there was a paved bike path all the way. I didn't have to hurry, because Wanda said she'd be staying home all day even if Angie got sick again. For a change, the weather was mild and sunny. I decided it'd be a good time to get a look at the swans up close.

As I walked along, I tried to figure out what I'd say to Cooper Davis if he was still there. It shouldn't be a big problem; I mean, even though he wrote poetry and had a mashed nose, he probably couldn't be all that much different from Vinnie, right?

Then I was sort of surprised to realize I'd never actually talked all that much to my brother, which meant I didn't have a lot of practice with boys that age. Sure, Vinnie and I were brother and sister, which would make a person think we were close. I liked to think of all the Reillys being like peas in a pod, but things can keep people apart. Like, Vinnie was heavy into being your basic, famous High School Hero, but I was always someone in the background. Only a middle kid in middle school, not famous for anything special. As far as Vinnie was concerned, I was, well, just there.

Cooper Davis was raking up some stuff as I came up alongside the fence that kept the swans from wandering onto the highway. His notebook was nestled snugly in my pocket. I hooked my fingers on the chain links of the fence, and waited for some cool greeting to jump into my mind. None did.

"Hey, Cooper," I called finally. He whirled around as if I'd said, "Raise your hands—this is a stickup!"

I held up the notebook. "You left this on the bus the other day," I said.

He laid the rake on the ground and walked slowly toward me. I was glad the fence was between him and me, because to be honest there was something sort of spooky about him. His eyes were long and narrow, neither light nor dark, and tilted up at the outer corners; he didn't look anything like the guys Vinnie hung out with. Maybe he *was* different; Vinnie and his buddies always had everything they ever wanted, but hard times were written all over Cooper Davis in bold, black letters. He looked like someone who didn't know a single thing about being a famous High School Hero.

"You were the last one off the bus that day," he snapped, as if I'd planned it that way just so I could steal his stupid notebook. I pitched it over the top of the fence. He caught it, then took a couple steps back.

"I go out to the prison every Saturday," I said. "I always ride at the back." I paused. A week ago, I'd thought it would be easy to talk to him because we had something in common. Up close, I decided I'd made a big mistake.

"Little squirt like you?" I knew exactly what I saw in his eyes. *Somebody's skinny kid sister,* he was thinking.

"Who you know out there?" he asked bluntly, and nodded over his shoulder in the direction of the FDC.

"My dad. And I'm not a squirt." We studied each other warily through the fence, like animals at a zoo. "I guess you know someone out there, just like me," I said. I heard a quivery, scared sound in my voice, and pointed at his notebook.

In the story I'd invented, Cooper Davis's brother had been caught somewhere with a stash of drugs worth millions of dollars. The judge had said, "We're going to get scumbags like you off the streets and keep you off. You're a menace to society.'' His brother would be what some people called a blue-collar criminal, the type most folks think about as being the worst kind.

Cooper Davis cradled the book in his palm. I expected him to scowl, but instead he gave me a quirky smile. It was sort of a Skipper-type smile, shy, and a little embarrassed. ''Whoa! Where'd you get the idea I knew anyone at the prison?'' he asked.

''That poem you wrote,'' I said, pointing at the notebook again. ''About pigeons and prisoners. I figured you must know a prisoner out there, too.''

He studied me with narrow wolf eyes. ''Listen, kid, not all prisons are made out of bricks or stone. The reason I ride the prison bus sometimes is because it's a handy way to get out here in a hurry.'' He gestured toward the pond, at the swans. ''When I'm done feeding these dumb birds, I go back to town where I've got another job.'' I noticed he didn't mention anything about school.

''You don't exactly look like a person who'd write poems,'' I said, even though I realized a poet could be just like anybody.

Cooper David raised his eyebrows. ''How do you think one ought to look?'' he demanded.

I didn't answer his question. ''My dad will probably be getting out pretty soon,'' I said instead, since the topic of poems seemed to be a touchy one with him. My remark surprised me more than it did Cooper Davis. As yet, my dad hadn't told me anything about what I was supposed to do to help him get a new hearing, one that would lead to his being released sooner than any of us expected.

''There was a mistake at the first trial,'' I rattled on.

"My dad's innocent; he even told me so. It's only a matter of time till I'll be able to help him prove it. I think he's got some evidence stashed somewhere. You know, records, documents, tape recordings, stuff like that." To list the evidence aloud made it seem so real, I could actually see it: printouts with lots of numbers, manila folders stuffed full of information, cassettes neatly labeled. CONFERENCE WITH E. M. ENDERSEN, JUNE 12TH. Stuff like that.

Cooper Davis raised his eyebrows again, then turned to squint in the direction of the FDC, where both of us could see the rolls of razor wire on top of the prison fence gleam in the spring sun. From a distance there was no way to tell how sharp those razors were, but Dad told me they were like a piranha's teeth, that they could chew the meat right off a man's bones if he ever took a notion to escape.

I turned my eyes away. Behind Cooper, the white swans floated calmly on the black water, their necks curved and as graceful as the letter *S. Swans and razor wire* . . . my old life had been so simple; I'd never had to make painful comparisons.

"I bet most of the guys out there don't want to admit they're guilty of anything," Cooper mused.

"But my dad's not guilty," I insisted. "I already told you that." Those two words, *not guilty,* were ones I never had to puzzle over. They were as much a part of me as my own skin, and just as important for keeping me glued together. As soon as I said them to the guy on the other side of the fence, though, one of those humps settled into the conversation I was trying to have with him, just like it did when I tried to talk to Dad. There was no way I could talk to Cooper Davis, either; there was no use pretending.

"Hey, kid, maybe I'll see you next week," he called after me in a beseeching Skipper-type voice when I turned to leave. I pretended not to hear, and just kept walking back toward Burnsville.

It was a downer not to have anyone to talk to, though, so as soon as I got back to Wanda's I went straight upstairs and wrote a letter to Vinnie. I'd written to him a couple times, but he'd never answered. No doubt he was too busy carving out a big new hero career for himself.

"Today I met a guy about your age," I reported. "He rides the same bus out to the FDC that I do. He writes poems about pigeons and prisoners. He doesn't look much like a poet, though. But you want to know what he told me? That not all prisons are made out of bricks or stone. So, Vinnie, I need your opinion. Does he sound kind of weird, or what? Please write back as soon as you can, okay?"

I reread what I'd written, then crumpled up the page. For sure Vinnie didn't want to hear anything about poems or prisons. My brother was busy trying to forget, not remember.

I decided to call Louise instead. Ramona said I could, anytime I wanted to, and gave me permission to call collect so Wanda wouldn't be stuck with any extra charges on her phone bill, which she warned me she couldn't afford on the kind of tips she made at the Sup-R-Chef. I hoped Louise would answer, but after four rings it was Ramona who did.

"Louise just left," she apologized. "There's a basketball game this afternoon and she's working with the Booster Club—you know, selling Cokes and popcorn and candy bars from one of those cute little stands with a striped awning."

I didn't know anything about popcorn or striped awnings. Louise had never been much for clubs before, partly because she was sort of self-conscious about being a little chubby.

"Kenwood's playing Fremont for the district championship," Ramona explained. "Do you want me to have her call you back tomorrow, Glennis?"

"Forget it," I said, "I was just touching base." I was glad Ramona didn't ask me anything personal. Such as, "How are things going for *you,* Glennis?", because I might have broken down and told her the truth before I could stop myself.

"They're going awful," I would have admitted. I probably would've cried, too. "I'm lonely here and I don't have any friends and I think maybe I'm sorry I asked for Wanda after all."

That's what I might have said if I'd detected the least little note of sympathy in Ramona's voice. But all she said was, "I'll tell Louise you called, dear." She sounded hopelessly cheerful, and I knew she was in heaven because now, at last, she had a real live teenager of her own.

There was another reason I was glad I didn't have a chance to confess anything to Ramona. A slip like that would've made me feel as if I'd been disloyal to my dad. That's something I'd vowed never to do. This moment of weakness would pass. I mean, hadn't I made up my mind to be the one who waited? Absolutely. I was Glennis, the one who had made a vow to be faithful to the end. What I hadn't counted on was that it would be so hard. That my old life seemed to get farther and farther away instead of coming closer and closer.

🌹 Chapter Six

I told Dad the truth when I said school was okay, that people were getting used to me and I was getting used to them.

For instance, it was a big relief that nobody stared at me anymore when I walked into Mrs. McCarthy's room. Once in a while, one of the girls even smiled and waggled her fingers in my direction. Sometimes, a boy named Adam Brusky looked at me as if he wanted to say, "Hi," maybe even add something stupid and familiar, like, "How about a game of tennis, Glennis?" but was too timid to actually get the words out. Mostly, I just minded my own business and kept my eyes down. Anybody would've thought my Reeboks were the most fascinating things I'd ever seen.

Then it happened.

"Want to eat with me and Karalyn today?" Mary Carpenter asked with a big smile when the third-period lunch bell rang on Monday. She sat one row over and two seats in front of me.

I swallowed hard.

After a Saturday at the prison, on Mondays my skin still felt thin, as if it were as transparent as tissue paper. I was afraid people could see right into me, would be able to read all about my secret life as if it were a headline in a newspaper.

"Uh . . . sure." She seemed a little surprised that I didn't act more thrilled by the invitation. I realized that after a lot of finger-waggling, Mary and her friends had finally decided I was all right, that it was okay to be nice to me. From my point of view, being accepted meant complications loomed on the horizon. It didn't take long for one of them to show up, either.

"We're having a sleepover Friday night at my place," Karalyn announced as soon as we all got our trays loaded and sat down. "Mary's coming, and so is LuAnn. Maybe even Janet." Karalyn smiled, too. It was obviously a big day for smiles. "So I was wondering, Glennis, d'you want to come over? My mom doesn't mind having a house full for supper."

I studied my taco salad, then piled all the olives against one edge of the shell. They were my favorite part, so I always saved them for last.

"Hey, I'd really like to," I said. "But I've always got to baby-sit my cousin Skipper first thing Saturday morning. See, he's only seven and too little to be left alone." Naturally, I never mentioned the FDC.

The smile I gave back to them was a low-voltage kind. "But listen, if my aunt ever changes jobs and doesn't have to work weekends anymore, then maybe sometime I could . . ."

It was plain that both Mary and Karalyn were disappointed. LuAnn just shrugged as if she never really wanted me to sleep over in the first place. For the rest of lunch the three of them talked mostly to each other, and although I usually like taco salad a lot, I hardly ate half of mine. Would you believe, not even all the olives.

When we got back to class that afternoon, Mrs. McCarthy announced our next English project. The one we'd just finished was journal writing. When we started it, she told us our entries would be kept strictly confidential, but just to be on the safe side I invented a make-believe life for her to read about.

"My sister's name is Laura," I wrote in one entry. "She's always been the apple of my mother's eye. My mother is a famous New York model—you've probably seen her picture in magazines—and she always wears pale, tasteful colors, especially one called taupe. When my parents got divorced" (I got interested in the story myself as I wrote it), "my mother took Laura, who is skinny and terribly nervous, away to live with her in a penthouse apartment overlooking Central Park. No one wanted me" (it wasn't true, but I liked this part the best), "so I ended up with a black sheep relative named Wendi, who lives on the east side of Burnsville, over there near the railroad tracks, and who's got a little boy named Scooter. My dad, who's a well-known nature photographer, left last month to chart an unexplored branch of the Amazon River. He'll be gone a long time, but when he gets back, he'll write a book that will be published by the National Geographic Society. It will probably be made into a TV documentary, too. Be sure to look for his name in the credits, Jason Vincent Reilly."

Mrs. McCarthy was impressed. "My, you certainly have an unusual background, Glennis!" she wrote in green ink in the margin. Just exactly how unusual I didn't intend for her to ever find out.

"Writing isn't the only way we communicate," Mrs. McCarthy told us on Monday afternoon. I thought she looked at me with special attention. "In fact, it's not the way we communicate most of the time. Usually, we speak to each other, in person and on the phone and so forth, don't we, class?"

Everyone nodded, and I shuddered to think what might come next.

"There are two kinds of speech that we use," Mrs. McCarthy said. A couple of boys in the corner snickered, then started to cluck like chickens and flap their elbows up and down.

"That will do, Dennis," Mrs. McCarthy cautioned. "You, too, Grady. Now, class, we use what is called casual speech for conversations with our friends and families. But we use a more formal type of speech when we appear before larger groups, don't we?"

A few mouths dropped. I felt myself shrink in my seat.

"In the next fifteen minutes," Mrs. McCarthy went on, "I want each of you to make a list of things you'd like to make a speech about. Later, I will review the lists with each of you privately. Then you'll begin to work on a speech to present to the class toward the end of the semester."

She looked pleased, as if she really looked forward to what we were all about to do. "Some of you might wish to explore an important community issue," she suggested. "For example, recycling or the need for a new animal shelter or the importance of low-cost child care, while some of you might decide to share some particular aspect about yourselves or your families."

Everybody in the room started to buzz—you know how it is when everyone gets ready to start a new project like that—and Mrs. McCarthy tapped her knuckles against her desk to get our attention. "Quiet, class—and please start your lists now. I'd like you to hand them in before you leave at the end of the period."

The sheet of notebook paper in front of me looked as desolate as a Siberian wasteland. My mission, I decided, was to get across that vast snowscape without leaving any footprints. I started my list.

1. Why too much violence on TV is bad for impressionable kids.
2. How to decorate a room that has old, unzipped wallpaper.
3. Why cats make ideal pets, even if they're elderly, like Sugar.
4. The natural history of swans.

My list was more interesting for what it omitted than for what it contained. Nowhere was there any mention of why I took a bus ride every Saturday to the FDC, what had happened to Rags, or the awful time my mother was having at Fair Haven. Nothing about the twins, Vinnie, Louise, or the Sterling Savings and Loan.

You might want to share some particular aspect about yourselves or your families, Mrs. McCarthy had suggested. Get real. Personal was the last thing I would ever be.

On Saturday, I noticed Dad had dark circles under his eyes. I imagined him tossing and turning all night on a narrow prison cot that was hard as a board. Maybe it *was* a board, with only a thin blanket folded in half for a mattress.

When I hugged him, his backbone was knobbier than

ever, like a piece of rope with knots tied in it every inch or so. I made a fresh vow: I'd learn how to bake, just like Mrs. Cinnamon Buns. Every weekend from now on I'd bring him out something special to eat that would put meat back on his bones.

"Glennis, let's sit over here in the corner," Dad suggested. "Where we can really talk." He seemed jittery, and a blue vein in his jaw flickered and jumped under his skin, which was pale now that he'd lost all his tennis tan.

We sat across from each other over a card table that other prisoners sometimes used for playing Monopoly or Scrabble during Saturday visits. Dad leaned his elbows on the table and bent toward me.

"I know what you've been thinking, Glennis," he said.

"You do?" I was awfully surprised. It was true my speech had been on my mind practically every minute since Mrs. McCarthy announced our new assignment, but it was only yesterday that we'd agreed the topic about swans would be a good choice. ("Probably very few of your classmates know much about such birds," she'd pointed out.)

How could Dad have guessed all that? I was glad, though, because it just showed that deep down we knew each other very well. We were the kind of people who didn't always need to put every little thing into words.

"You know what's so special about you, Glennis?"

I waited for him to tell me. The expression in his eyes seemed unusually tender, and was tinged with regret.

"You're the one who's really been here for me. Everyone else has kept their distance, even Nana—not that I blame anybody for that, you understand. But you've been the steady one. A true believer. That's how I think

45

of you, Glennis. So steady and loyal that I think none of us ever realized how special you've always been."

The minute he said those words, the visitors' lounge began to glow. In the shafts of sunlight that came through the dirt-streaked windows high above us, particles of dust glistened like tiny bits of gold. I felt as if I were in a cathedral, as if I'd just been blessed. Everything was worth it to have him say I was special—living in a cramped room in Wanda's attic, inventing fake stories to put in my journal so Mrs. McCarthy would never know anything about the real me—it was all worth it.

Then my dad smiled ruefully. "You're a real rock, you know, just like your grandmother."

He was right about Nana being a rock, which was good, I suppose, but it also meant she could be as unmovable as a boulder. I'd had to argue (I even sniffled a little, almost had to get down on my knees and beg) before I was allowed to go live with Wanda, and my grandmother gave her permission only after she had long private talks with everyone in the whole family. Except my mother, of course, who was already at Fair Haven by then.

"Vinnie hated everything that happened," Dad went on, "and I can understand that. This is such an important time in a boy's life. He'd always been the hero son of a hero dad, and when that foundation cracked—well, Glennis, I don't blame him for never writing to me."

"I'll get on his case," I promised, and felt my cheeks get hot. Darn that Vinnie! The only person my brother ever seemed to think about was his own famous, wonderful self. Now I was pretty sure it hadn't really been worry that I saw in Vinnie's eyes the day I asked for Wanda.

"Louise has always been so shy, maybe even shyer than you," Dad went on. Was she? I'd always thought of my sister as being quiet, which is different from being shy. "I never knew for sure exactly how Louise felt," he murmured. I decided not to tell him that now, living with Ramona and Robert, Louise admitted she felt special for the first time in her life and had joined the Booster Club.

"And the twins," Dad said, sighing. "Well, I try to convince myself maybe they're too young to have been damaged as badly as you older kids have been by everything that happened."

He looked at me so steadily I couldn't have peeled my glance away even if I'd wanted to, which, of course, I didn't. He talked about each of us as if we were survivors of some kind of war, and I suppose the reason he never mentioned my mother was because it hurt him too much to think about where she was now.

His brown eyes got darker, darker. Slowly, the smile in them faded. Once again, I felt myself being lowered down, down into their depths. Dad's expression became so serious that my heart and head felt like I'd just hit the Pause button on a TV remote control. Everything stopped. Dad slid his hands across the table and covered mine with them.

"Glennis, I want to tell you something I've never told anyone else. Not my lawyers. Not your mother. Not your grandmother. No one. But now it's critically important for *you* to know it, just because you're the sort of steady, loyal person you are."

I was filled up with something so rare, so delicious I could actually taste it on the tip of my tongue. Tart, but sweet, too, like the raspberries we picked every summer in the sunny meadow behind my grandparents' house near the lake.

I knew I'd been right! I leaned toward him, eager for what he was finally ready to tell me. He'd made up his mind to give me instructions about where to find a certain secret key. It flashed through my mind he'd hidden it in back of that framed picture of the whole family that I kept on the rickety night table in Wanda's upstairs bedroom.

He'd tell me to take the velvet back off the picture, and remove the key from where he'd taped it in place. Next, he'd direct me to an airport locker. He'd been free on bond all during the trial, so he would have had time to take documents to a crowded, busy place like New York or San Francisco, where it would be easier to hide important stuff from enemies who'd threatened the lives of his wife and children.

Most likely I'd have to ask for some extra money from Nana for the trip. I'd have to make sure all my underwear was clean. I'd wear Mom's vanilla-colored sweater. In the airport locker I would find all the evidence needed to ask for a new trial. When we finally took back the life that belonged to us, everyone in the family would forget how awful the past year had been. We would buy our old house back; Rags could come home again; all the stuff about the trial would fade like a dream you can't remember in the morning.

My father's hands were warm and steady on top of mine, and I waited for him to go on.

"Glennis, I committed every crime the prosecution claimed I did," I said.

His eyes were dark and bottomless. I tumbled over the edge, and fell all the way down.

"I'm not taking a rap for anyone, Glennis," he said.

His voice was quiet, matter-of-fact. When I crashed to the bottom, I felt every bone in my body crack.

"At the trial, they said I lied. *I did,* Glennis."

I stared at him. "But I thought Mr. Endersen—"

"They said I stole other people's money," he interrupted, and there was a hard, cold note in his voice. "*I did,* Glennis."

"If he hadn't been holding my hands, I would have covered my ears so I wouldn't hear anything else.

"*I'm guilty,* Glennis. I don't want you to believe for one more day—*not for one more second*—that I'm innocent. I'm not. That's what you've got to understand, Glennis. The sentence the judge handed down to me was fair. Your dad wasn't anybody's victim, only his own. But I'm not going to allow you to be a victim, too."

My hands turned to ice under his warm ones. I took them back and stuck my fists under my armpits. I should have said something, but the only word that came out was, "Why?"

"I didn't intend to do harm, Glennis," he explained. "But it was a time of mergers, buyouts, high inflation— all of which made the chance to cash in on certain investment opportunities irresistible. Brokers and big-money people all over the country—even in out-of-the-mainstream cities like Kenwood—were doing exactly the same thing." He paused, as if marveling how easy it had been.

"Fortunes were being made by men who weren't any smarter than I was, Glennis." I knew I'd never be a Bunny again.

"It meant huge potential profits, and security for the entire SS&L. It meant a better life for all of us. I never suspected any of the deals I made would go so sour. I didn't realize I was weaving a web that would trap not only me, but everyone I loved.''

Except there was no reason for him to weave webs. Our life had been okay the way it was. It didn't need to be better. Our house had four bathrooms. We all had our own bedrooms, except the twins, who always wanted to be together anyway. A man came to take care of the lawn and flowers once a week. My mother had a part-time housekeeper named Bernice. I had horseback riding lessons; Louise took piano; the twins had dance class; Vinnie went to expensive sport camps every summer. Best of all, the Reillys had each other. None of us needed anything else.

No announcement came over the loudspeaker, but I got up anyway. "I've got to go now," I said. On other Saturdays I always added, "See you next week." This time I didn't.

Outside, I climbed on the bus. "How you doin' today, girlie?" the grandpa driver asked, his gentle blue eyes twinkling in their crepe-paper nests. I didn't answer, just headed straight for the back of the bus. At terrible moments, a person thinks of weird things. Like, now I wouldn't have to learn how to bake. I didn't care if my dad got as thin as a pin. He could starve, for all I cared.

I didn't look for the swans as we passed the park. My face felt numb, like after you've been to the dentist and have been pumped full of Novocain. My ears rang. My hands were still freezing.

I'd given up my brother and sisters, my old room in a tall white house on a hill, all my friends, without complaining—not even when Rags went away—because I knew in my heart that *my dad was innocent.*

Now, he'd committed two crimes. The one he was in prison for, and the one he committed today when he trashed my faith. At Wanda's block, I got off the bus. I walked up the street, stiff as a robot. What would I do now that I knew Dad was really, truly a crook? Had robbed widows and orphans of their life savings? I didn't have a clue.

The only thing I knew for sure was now it was me who was adrift on an ice floe in some endless Arctic night. It was me who couldn't make myself heard in the freezing darkness.

❧ Chapter Seven

*T*he next Saturday I didn't get up early. Instead, I stayed in bed until I heard the bus go by in front of Wanda's house.

What kind of treats had Mrs. Cinnamon Buns baked today? Did the Movie Star have a deal in Hollywood yet? Had the Godfather traded his beautiful winter coat for a light spring one? Was Cooper Davis frowning at his grumpy reflection in the dusty window?

A guilty conscience, heavy as a rain-soaked sleeping bag on a Girl Scout camp-out, weighed me down. It was the first Saturday since I'd move to Burnsville that I hadn't gone to the FDC. I listened to the sound of the bus grow fainter as it moved down the block, and held my hands over my heart. It felt bruised and battered, like a homing pigeon that's made a long flight through a terrible hailstorm.

There were some old water stains on the ceiling of Wanda's spare room. I squinted at them. Was there a secret message hidden in those rusty dots and squiggles telling me what I ought to do next? Whether I should ever go back to the prison or dump my dad just like everyone else in the family had, including my grandmother, who wrote to him sometimes but never came to visit? If the message was there I couldn't decode it, so finally I got up.

"You still here?" Skipper asked, surprised, when I clumped downstairs. "I think you missed your bus, Glen."

"It's okay, Skipper," I said, yawning and trying to act natural. "I'm not going today. Something else came up."

"Something else? Like what?" Suddenly, the little turkey was on fire with curiosity. He turned off the TV, and plucked at the hem of my sweatshirt when he came to stand beside me. Was it only two weeks ago I'd given him a lecture about ruining his delicate mental health by spending too much time in front of the boob tube? Now I would've paid him to quit bugging me, to get lost in some stupid cartoon about homicidal cats and stressed-out mice.

"Homework," I said, glad it wasn't exactly a lie. "I've got this important project for my English class. I'm going to work on it today."

He followed me into the kitchen and watched me warm up a bowl of milk for Sugar. "When you get finished, maybe we could all do something together," he suggested. "You and me and Mom. You know, sort of like we were a real family." I could see the idea appealed to him a whole bunch.

What I could tell him about a real family was everything he didn't need to know. Mothers have nervous breakdowns, and brothers and sisters end up being strangers to each other. Worst of all, fathers tell lies that ruin a person's life. But Skipper was only in second grade; I figured he'd learn soon enough how terrible the world can be without any help from me.

"So what do you want to do?" I asked.

"You pick," he offered generously.

I thought of my unzipped walls upstairs. "Umm. Your mom said she might fix up my room. After I do some homework, and after she gets up, maybe we could go downtown and buy some paint. Then we could have lunch somewhere, and when we come back here you and me could rip off all that ugly old wallpaper up there. You want to help tear paper off the walls, Skipper?"

His eyes gleamed with fiendish delight. The idea of making a big mess without getting blamed for it pleased him. He zoomed around the kitchen, making horrible shredding noises, while I got out the cornflakes and mixed up a pitcher of powdered orange juice.

He made such a racket that Wanda didn't get to sleep in as late as usual, so while she made coffee we talked to her about going downtown. She hadn't combed her hair yet, which was as spiky as Skipper's, and her mascara was all smudgy, making her look more exhausted than ever. I knew she'd been working too many extra shifts lately.

"I'll have to check my budget first," she warned. "Nothing's cheap these days, you know. Paint can be real pricey stuff, which explains why I haven't gotten around to painting the outside of the house since we moved in."

"I've got my allowance money," I said. Nana sent it to me twice a month, and now that I wasn't a mall rat anymore, I'd saved practically every nickel of it. "I'll buy the paint, okay?" Wanda looked relieved, and I thought how lucky my mom had always been: Before my dad went to prison, she'd never had to worry about not having money, or ever needed to work extra shifts at anything.

There were so many colors to choose from at the Paint 'n' Paper store, I hardly knew where to begin choosing. "What sort of exposure does the room have?" the salesman finally asked Wanda, a question that made my aunt turn a little pink.

"The room we're talking about, young man, isn't exposed," she said indignantly. "It has all its walls and everything. A window with glass in it. Even a screen in summer."

"What I mean, ma'am, is does it face east or west or north or south," he explained, turning pink himself. "That's what decorators mean when they say exposure."

"East," I said, because I woke up every morning to see the sun peeking through a hole in the window shade.

He helped us pick out some colors that would be appropriate—peach and pink and something mauve-y, about the shade of the dusty stuff on a just-ripe plum. "This won't take a minute," he said, and turned to a machine that mixed up the paint for us.

When it was done—we agreed on a shade named Peach Parfait—we left the store and went to a place called Burger Bonanza because Wanda said she couldn't stand to eat where she had to work every day, that she'd memorized the menu and all the smells, which she said were truly disgusting. We had cheeseburgers, fries, and frosted malts, and when the bill came I chipped in from my allowance so it wouldn't wreck her budget.

When we got up to leave, a busboy in a green jacket came from the kitchen to clear off the table. When he got up close, I could see he had narrow wolf eyes and a mashed nose.

"Hello, kid," he said, surprised as I was. His voice was husky, like a movie actor's. "You sleep in this morning, or what? I missed you." He gave me a wink, as if we shared some kind of secret.

Wanda's black eyebrows flew up like a pair of jet planes to attack her spiky platinum bangs. That remark, *I missed you*, really got her attention. Skipper stared at Cooper as if he'd never seen a teenage boy before, then at me as if he wasn't sure he knew who I was anymore.

"Uh, I had stuff to do," I mumbled. At least I knew now where he got all the bread and lettuce he carried out to feed the swans. As we walked home, of course, Wanda wasted no time getting on my case.

"Now, Glennis, I realize I'm not your mother, but I'm responsible for you while you live with me," she began. I could see she took the job seriously, but I was relieved that she actually seemed more worried than mad. "Your grandmother Reilly would absolutely have kittens, a dozen of 'em, if she knew you'd gotten chummy with a boy like that. I'm sure you realize he's not the sort of person she'd approve of at all, Glennis, not to mention that he's—"

"Got creepy eyes!" Skipper put in, his voice squeaky with alarm. "He looks sort of"—he hooked a finger in the corner of his mouth and searched for the right word, as if it were hidden in his bicuspids—"dangerous!" he yelped.

"I think he's about Vinnie's age," I said, as if that explained something important, which I knew perfectly well it didn't. "And I'm sure he's not dangerous. His name's Cooper Davis, and he, um, writes poetry."

"That's not necessarily any guarantee of a sound character," Wanda warned me. "You're not even thirteen yet, Glen. A boy like that could sweet-talk a kid like you into practically anything.''

She said *anything* with special emphasis, and raised her eyebrows again. "I don't think you'd better see him anymore, hon.'' She leaned close and whispered in my ear, so Skipper wouldn't hear.

"Lemme tell you, Glen, I could recite you chapter and verse about guys who talk sweet, and the kind of trouble it can get a nice girl into.''

"I don't *see* him, not the way you mean,'' I objected. "Like you just said, Wanda, I'm not even thirteen yet. I'm too young for that stuff. Look, I only ride the same bus he does on Saturday morning. I don't even sit with him. He stays close to the front—I go way to the back and sit by myself. Honest.''

"Just promise you'll keep your distance from boys like him,'' Wanda pleaded.

"Okay, okay. I promise.''

By then we were home, and Skipper was hot to start ripping paper off the walls upstairs, so we tackled the job right away. Since it was old and dry, most of it came off real easy. What was left we scraped off with a spatula I got from the kitchen.

"We can start to paint next weekend, if you want,'' Wanda suggested when Skipper and I finally went back downstairs. I was glad that she seemed to have put the wolf man out of her mind. She was frying chicken for supper, something she'd never done all the time I'd lived in Burnsville. Skipper, whose hair was sprinkled with shredded yellow roses, couldn't keep from smiling.

"Just think, all of us were together the whole day, and now Momma's making fried chicken from scratch,'' he said. My cousin had absolutely fallen in love with stuff made from scratch. "After, we can watch TV. It's always funner when there's someone to watch with."

Wanda stopped mashing potatoes and stared at him, her eyes round with surprise. "I didn't know you minded watching TV alone," she said.

"I do!" Skipper exclaimed. "Because it's lonesome, that's why. I bet it could even ruin a person's delicate mental health!" His words were loaded with enough reproach to keep his mother awake every night for a week. That's when I realized maybe Wanda and Skipper didn't know each other much better than it turned out my own family did.

Which, in a way, made it seem not so horrible that I planned to talk to Cooper Davis again just as soon as I got the chance. Because when Mrs. McCarthy agreed with me that the class might be interested in a speech about the natural history of swans, she also pointed out it would be nice if I could consult with a resource person, someone who knew a lot about such birds. She seemed pleased when I told her I knew someone exactly like that.

What was really on my mind, though, was Cooper Davis knew something important about prisons. Maybe he knew other things, too. Like what a person should do when they found out the person they loved best had told a lie that was bigger than the whole world.

My main problem was, had my dad lied to me? Had he ever asked me to believe he was innocent?

No.

Right from the start that was my own idea, right? Right. So what I needed to do was figure out a way to handle the fact that now I knew he deserved to be right where he was: in prison. For ten whole years, if that's how it turned out.

🌺 Chapter Eight

*I*t was raining when the bus stopped at the corner, and I could see Cooper's sour face, wavy and green, through the glass. This time I didn't go all the way to the back of the bus; instead, I plopped myself on the seat right beside him. On the floor between us was a large white plastic bucket full of lettuce and bread.

"How come you ride all the way out to the prison, then turn around and walk back to the park?" I asked.

He winked slyly, and seemed not so sullen after all. A guy never winked at me before; it made me a little nervous to think about Wanda's warning, that somebody like him could be bad news for a person my age. "So I can smell whatever it is that lady carries out in that white box," he said, and nodded toward Mrs. Cinnamon Buns. "It smells, you know, warm and homey. My ma wasn't much into that kinda stuff." He gave me a no-big-deal smile.

"Well, if it's okay, I'll walk back with you," I said, to give him a chance to say no if he didn't want company.

"Whoa—aren't you going to see your old man today?" he asked, surprised. I'd never thought of my dad as an old man; mostly, I thought about him as a grown-up version of the golden boy my grandparents once loved so well. Whom *I* also once loved so well.

Cooper looked straight at me. Naturally I had to look back. No matter what Skipper's opinion was, his eyes didn't seem dangerous. They were a funny shade of blue and gray and brown all mixed together, sort of like that taupe color my grandmother was so crazy about. Behind them, I thought I saw a person who maybe wasn't much older than I was myself.

I shook my head. "I can't today. I've got too much homework," I told him. "See, I've got to make this speech at school. I decided to give one about swans." I couldn't put into words the true reason I wanted to talk to him.

"And the reason I'm on this bus this morning is, well, maybe you could tell me stuff about 'em. My teacher said it would be a good thing to have a resource person. Someone who's had firsthand experience with such birds. You know, who can tell me what some of their weird habits are and stuff like that."

Cooper lifted one shoulder in a vaguely pleased, older-brother shrug. I figured it was his way of agreeing we had ourselves a deal.

The rain had quit by the time we got to the FDC, so we headed back toward the park on an asphalt bike path dappled with blotches of April sun and shadow. I wondered if there was any way my dad could see us from one of those high windows in the visitors' lounge. If, at this very moment, he was watching me walk away, never once looking back over my shoulder. Would he be disappointed that, for the second Saturday in a row,

I hadn't come through the door with everyone else who got off the bus? Something in me hoped he *was* watching, wanted him to feel brokenhearted just like I was when he admitted he was a crook.

"So you want to know about swans for your speech." Cooper gave me a sharp look, "Say, kid, what grade you in, anyway?"

When I told him, he said he'd been ripping off candy bars and pop from convenience stores when he was my age. Which made me wonder if maybe Skipper was partly right about his eyes.

"But, hey, you don't want to hear exciting tales about my life of crime, right? You want to find out something about swans." It seemed to puff him up, knowing he was going to be somebody's resource person. "Well, until a few months ago, a swan was just a big, dumb white bird as far as I was concerned. I didn't care diddly about 'em." My grandmother would have called his language coarse and common. She would've been right; it was. It made me a little nervous to think maybe I was adding a fresh mistake to that long string I'd been making lately . . . pretending people were something they weren't.

"After I started doing this job, though, I realized there's just something about these birds. When they're in the water, you think you've never seen anything more graceful—then you see 'em on land and you realize they've got that other clumsy, klutzy side. Two sides, just like people, sort of a light side and a dark side. So that's when I started to read up on 'em."

A light side and a dark side. I liked how that sounded. As we walked along, the bucket of food bonked against his leg, then against mine.

To start with, Cooper told me it took thirty days for

cygnets to hatch out. "That's what a baby swan is called," he explained. "Chicks are what chickens hatch out, goslings are hatched by a goose, and cygnets are what swans hatch out. And that's a good time to be pretty careful around the parent birds," he warned.

"See, a swan will use its wings as if they're weapons, like a pair of clubs. In this one book I read it said that a drake—a male swan—broke a man's shinbone because he accidentally got too close to a nesting site. They're very territorial, and super-protective of their young."

What was my dad doing when he should've been protecting his young? Trying to make bigger profits. So we could all have more stuff

"Swans usually mate for life," Cooper went on, so serious and eager to tell me everything he knew; I smiled when I imagined how pleased Mrs. McCarthy would be with him. "Sometimes, one of 'em will even die of heartbreak if their partner gets killed." He told me there's a special oil gland that keeps a swan's feathers waterproof, that sometimes a drake can weigh as much as fifty pounds, that in England swans are protected by an order from the queen. I hoped I'd be able to remember everything he told me.

When we got to the pond, I watched Cooper throw out bread and lettuce to the waiting birds. He was right in the middle of telling me that some swans in Australia and New Zealand are black instead of white, when I heard myself yell in a loud voice that surprised me even more than it did him, "I just found out my dad's guilty!"

Cooper didn't look at me or say anything. He just kept right on pitching food to the birds.

"He did everything the newspapers said he did!" I rattled on, even louder.

"He lied and cheated and stole other people's money! Even from old people, widows, and orphans!"

Cooper emptied out the last tidbits, flipped the white bucket upside down, then sat on it. He turned, and looked at me hard. "That musta been pretty tough to listen to, kid," he said. His voice was gentle.

I leaned back against the fence. There was a weight in the pit of my stomach, the kind you get when you can't digest something.

I'd done what I'd pledged never to do: I'd broken my vow. I'd been disloyal and unfaithful. I hooked my fingers in the chain-link fence to keep from falling in a heap. Those words echoed in my ears. *He lied and cheated and stole other people's money.* I felt my skin get leaks in it; it wouldn't be able to hold me together much longer.

But all I could say was, "My name's not kid. It's Glennis. And don't pretend you're like a hundred years older'n me or anything. You're about the same age as my brother, Vinnie. Neither one of you guys is Methuselah." I took a deep breath. Since I'd already broken my vow, I decided to tell Cooper everything else there was to tell.

"There aren't any secret documents. No hidden keys. No airport lockers in San Francisco or New York that're full of evidence. There'll never be a new trial. We'll never get our old life back. My dad admitted he did everything everybody said he did." The nursery rhyme had it all right: No one could ever put Humpty Dumpty back together again.

I felt as horrible as the night the Mumfords drove off with Rags. The only thing that kept me from crying in front of Cooper Davis was that he didn't say anything too sympathetic.

"The truth is, I didn't come out here today to find out anything about swans. I mean, I could get all that out of a book, just like you did. What I really want to know is, well, what did you mean about prisons? About them not all being made out of bricks and stone?"

The look he finally gave me was long and careful. "I think you just found out, Glennis."

He hesitated, then clamped his hands together between his knees. "You know what I think?" I waited for him to tell me. "I think we build our own prisons, Glennis." He turned his gaze back to the swans. "Out of what we want to believe is true." I realized he was talking to himself as much as to me.

He'd said my name twice today, which made me feel peculiar, sort of like when Dad called me Bunny. I had the feeling Cooper knew exactly where I was coming from.

The swans finished their food and began to waddle back to the pond.

"So what am I supposed to do now?" There were no wailing police sirens in my voice anymore. "It wasn't supposed to be this way," I told Cooper. "I trusted my dad. He was special, not like other people. I loved him. To be honest, I guess I loved him better than Vinnie or Louise or the twins or even my mother. But now I think . . . maybe I hate him." My voice was dull and flat. The confession belonged to someone I didn't know anymore. Maybe it was the same thing Vinnie and my mother and everyone else had said: *I hate him.*

Cooper turned his not-dark, not-light wolf eyes back

to mine. This time, I knew he was seeing me, not somebody's skinny kid sister. He wasn't like Vinnie, who never actually saw me until all of us kids were about to get split up, when it was too late for anything to matter between us.

"The question you've gotta ask yourself, Glennis, are you gonna put yourself in jail because of what you just found out? Okay, so now you know your old man isn't exactly what you thought he was. Okay, so you're disappointed. Big deal. You gonna make him into something else he probably isn't? Like suddenly he's this blackhearted, worthless, no-good sleazebag? Remember what I said about the swans—that they've got a dark side and a light side?—well, sometimes people do, too. That doesn't necessarily make 'em monsters."

I studied the back of Cooper's neck, where his dark hair stuck out over the collar of his blue shirt. His hair wasn't exactly clean, and his collar was dirty. Louise would have turned up her nose; she would have said he looked scuzzy. Louise might not have any edges or angles, but she's just as picky as my grandmother in a lot of ways.

"So how come you know about stuff like this?" I asked. I was too tired to be mad anymore. All I wanted were answers.

"Did you ever wonder why I come out here every morning, Glennis?" He seemed bemused, and turned away again to look at the swans on the black water. "Because I dig swans? Not exactly. I'm doing community service, that's why. A hundred and fifty hours' worth. If you remember that poem, you probably remember the address that was in my notebook, right?"

It had been an odd one, a street number with the

initials P-O-R-T behind it. "Yeah—PORT—that's where I've lived for the past year. Stands for Probationed Offenders Rehabilitation Training. See, I got in trouble with a bunch of guys, and we trashed some windows at a car dealership, to the tune of a ton of money. The other guys were older'n me. Each one of 'em already had a record, so they got sent to a regular prison. I was a first-timer, underage besides, so I got stuck in PORT." He looked back at me.

"And this is one of the things I have to do to pay my debt—I feed a flock of birds every morning with leftovers from the Burger Bonanza, till finally I've done my hundred and fifty hours."

"But what about that poem?" I asked. "It was about pigeons, not swans."

"There were pigeons on the roof of the courthouse the day I got sentenced. After I got into PORT, I had to take a look at myself. Why I'd done what I did. You know what I think, Glennis? There's really not much difference between me and your dad. He did a big crime, I did a little one. Each one of us knew what we were doing was wrong—but we did it anyhow. So now it's payback time for him. For me, too."

This is what I'd wasted a whole Saturday morning to find out?

That now I knew two crooks? One with a white collar, another with a dirty blue one? One who stole money from old ladies, the other who trashed windows?

Talking to Cooper Davis wasn't going to help me. What I needed was a heart-to-heart talk with someone who'd been as wiped out by what happened to my Humpty Dumpty family as I was myself. A person whose spirit was broken just like mine, someone who might never be the same again. Once, she bought a vanilla-colored sweater in Ireland when she was on a second honeymoon with a person she trusted more than she trusted anybody in the world. My mother: a woman who was locked up in a different kind of prison than any of us, but it was a prison just the same.

❧ Chapter Nine

Wanda took a day of vacation from the Sup-R-Chef when I had a teacher's workday off at school, and we painted the bedroom upstairs. First, I helped her move all the dusty boxes of fabric scraps down into the living room, where she stacked them next to the TV.

"When I have time, I'm going to pitch all this stuff," she told me as she carried the last box down. "What have I been thinking all these years? That I would ever have the time or energy to make a quilt? Get real, Wanda Wayfield!" It was her third husband, Roman Wayfield, who was Skipper's dad. There was a snapshot of him in Skipper's room, but whoever took it had a shaky hand, and his face turned out sort of blurry.

We took turns with the paint roller, and when we were finished Wanda cleaned the windows and put up some new curtains almost the same peachy color as the walls. She put tape across the hole in the shade so the sun wouldn't shine in my eyes anymore.

"It looks really nice, Aunt Wanda," I told her. For

some dopey reason, I wanted to remind her she was my aunt. My flesh and blood. Maybe it was because I felt like I didn't have a father anymore, and with everyone else so far away I wanted to make sure she remembered we were kin. Of course, the room we'd just fixed up wasn't as fancy as my old one at home, where I had a white four-poster, dressers to match, and blue carpet I could sink up to my ankles in. What Wanda and I'd done, though, made this one look almost cozy.

"Good grief, Glen, quit with that dumb Aunt Wanda business!" she exclaimed, shaking her platinum hair out of her eyes. "It makes me sound like some awful, dowdy old lady!"

I hoped she'd keep her dowdy old lady remarks to herself if Nana ever came to visit, which, when I gave it a second thought, probably wasn't too likely. My grandmother's way of keeping in touch with me was to make sure my allowance checks were on time. Only once had she enclosed a personal note. "Let me know if you aren't happy at Wanda's," she wrote, "because other arrangements can always be made." Not that she suggested I come to her place on the lake—probably because she was too busy turning Vinnie into a carbon copy of my dad to even think of it.

I washed the paint roller in the kitchen sink while Wanda made some peppermint tea, and when we sat down she said she needed to have a serious talk with me.

She said *serious* and *talk* slowly, emphasizing each word as if it started with a capital letter. I felt my spine stiffen and the hairs on my neck get prickly. That's how people usually introduce unpleasant subjects. Maybe she'd found out about my meeting a week ago with

Cooper. I figured I was in for another your-grandmother-would-never-approve lecture.

"What I was wondering, Glen—well, hon, I won't futz around, but will just ask you point-blank. How come you never go out to visit your dad anymore?" She took a sip of tea and studied me thoughtfully. You know something? I was glad she asked. At least someone was thinking about me.

"I mean, isn't that why you came to live with me and Skipper in the first place? To be close to the prison? So I was wondering what—"

I'd only missed two Saturdays, but the way she asked made it sound like I'd defaulted on a whole month's worth of visits. She didn't know, of course, that it was Dad himself who'd been the first to say I shouldn't build my life around him. It wasn't *me* telling *him* that I shouldn't. Wanda didn't realize I was only taking the advice he gave me. What she didn't know was why, or that I wasn't sure if I wanted to see him again. Ever.

"I just decided I ought to concentrate on other stuff for a while," I said, and kept my words as vague as possible. I didn't plan to tell her Dad admitted he was guilty. Cooper Davis was the only one who knew that.

"Like, a while back I got asked to a sleepover by some girls at school, plus I figured I ought to try to get into more activities. Try to make some friends, you know." I could see Wanda wasn't convinced. "After all, I'll probably be here a long time; there's no sense pretending this is just for a while." Not that I was totally sure about the *for a while* part of my speech. Maybe I'd end up going to live with Ramona and Robert after all; they could have two princesses for the price of one. With my help, they would be twice as happy as they were now.

I'd already decided to do something else I hadn't mentioned to Wanda yet. Since it was her idea to have a serious talk, though, this seemed like the perfect time to drop the news on her.

"I've decided to go over to Fair Haven to see my mother," I announced.

Wanda frowned, and poured herself another cup of tea. "That's an awfully long trip," she pointed out. "I'm pretty sure I can't get off work to go with you, Glen. On the other hand, I'm not sure you ought to go by yourself. Sounds to me like another one of those things Nana Reilly definitely wouldn't approve of."

"It's not a big deal, Wanda. I already checked the bus schedules. A person doesn't have to transfer or anything; I'll be on one bus the whole way. I'll buy a round-trip ticket, and will come straight back. I promise not to get off to buy snacks or anything. Not to mention there's a bathroom right on the bus so I won't even have to get off for that."

Wanda felt so reassured she got a sudden bright idea. "Maybe Skipper could go with you, to sort of keep you company." Then she chewed on her lip. On second thought, it probably bothered her that my mother was at a place for treatment of emotional problems, that maybe Skipper shouldn't be exposed to what might go on there.

"But it's not as though Fair Haven is your garden-variety loony bin, not like a real mental hospital or anything like that," she reflected. I wished she hadn't used the phrase loony bin. "Being a private hospital, it's not over-crowded and is definitely upscale—your grandmother saw to that—so I guess I don't need to worry Skipper'll see stuff that might scare him."

I knew from having lived with Skipper for more than three months that he'd be crabby by the time we were three miles out of town. I couldn't think of worse company than him.

Besides, I'd already called Fair Haven, which was about a hundred and fifty miles away, and found out I could only visit for two hours. That meant I'd be able to take a morning bus over and the evening one back home. "It's okay," I said. "Maybe it's better if I go alone anyway." But as soon as I decided to visit my mother, something started to bug me so much I'd been having a hard time going to sleep at night. I decided to mention it to Wanda.

I wasn't sure what happened to people when they had nervous breakdowns. What if it meant everything got erased, like when you forget to press Save on your computer and end up losing everything you've got stored in random-access memory? I also wondered if she'd started to comb her hair yet, if she was interested in brushing her teeth again.

"Wanda, what if Mom doesn't remember me?" The thought made my stomach boil.

"Why, of course she'll remember you, Glen!" Wanda exclaimed. "She only had a breakdown, for heaven's sake. It's not like she has amnesia or anything like that. I know my own sister well enough to know she'll be real glad to see you." I decided maybe Wanda knew more about her sister than I knew about Louise.

The next Saturday, when usually I would've headed east to the FDC, I went west up the interstate toward Fair Haven. I slept most of the way, not because I was tired but because I didn't want to have to think about what I might find when I got there.

Wanda was right about my mother, though. She *was*

glad to see me, though it made my heart get a fresh, cracked feeling just to look at her.

Her brown hair was combed straight and plain (why hadn't I ever noticed it was practically the same color as mine?), but I didn't remember ever seeing any strands of gray in it before. She didn't wear the kind of makeup she used to, which once made her look almost like the sleek, famous New York model I'd invented for Mrs. McCarthy to read about.

"Why, Glennis," my mother said in a soft, tired voice. "My funny little girl in the middle, the one we all took for granted."

I'd thought no one had ever noticed, yet her words were almost the same ones Dad used! To realize she knew the same things about me that he did caused my nose to get that weird burny feel like just before you start to cry. I gritted my teeth to make sure I didn't. She folded me in her arms, and I realized she wasn't much taller than I was.

"Has it been okay for you here, Mom?" I asked when she let me go. Here I was, older than twelve, not quite thirteen, yet my mother and I actually had never been alone very much, just the two of us. It's not that she neglected any of us kids, like you hear some mothers who can afford housekeepers do, but it seemed like she was always so busy. And after Allie and Missy were born, she was busier than ever because she still kept up with all her volunteer work. And mother said that was an important part of being a member of your community.

My mother's visiting lounge wasn't much different from the one where Dad and I had met every Saturday. There were couches and chairs all around, in shades of lavender and gray, much prettier than the practical brown and black ones at the FDC. But that's not where my mother wanted to visit.

"Let's walk around the grounds," she said, smiling at me with careful, weary eyes. "This place deserves its name, Glennis. It's so restful, like places you see in English movies. There's even a little arched bridge that goes across a creek, sort of like the one we used to have in our backyard at home."

She took my hand as we walked along. Her fingers were slim and cool against mine. "The doctor says I'm getting better," she told me. "Just the same, I worry about how I'll feel when I get out." It was plain the prison she was in had gotten so comfortable she wasn't sure how soon she wanted to face the world again.

"Will you go back to Kenwood?" I asked. She'd have to get a different house, of course. A smaller one, because now there wasn't much money, only what was in a trust fund set up by my grandparents. She might even have to get a job. She'd probably have to do all her own housework. I could help, though, and so could Louise.

"I'm not sure, Glennis," my mother said, and sighed lightly. She brushed her straight gray-brown hair away from her cheek, and I noticed there was a pale circle around her finger where her wedding ring used to be. I hoped she'd taken it off only because she was so thin now it might fall off if she wore it.

"Maybe it would be a good idea to start over again someplace new," she murmured, and looked off across the misty treetops that dotted the manicured lawn at Fair Haven. "I've always thought I'd like to live in Albuquerque. It would be so different down there. There's a certain hot, dry cleanness about deserts, don't you think?"

It seemed strange to hear my mother say she'd always wanted to live some other place than where we'd always lived together. I never thought about her wanting anything except what all the rest of us did. About deserts—well, the only thing I knew about the ones in New Mexico was that they were a long way from the FDC. *But John Reilly is guilty,* a small voice reminded me. *You don't want to see him again, anyway.* So maybe it really didn't make much difference where we moved.

"Can I go with you, Mom?" She turned to me, her eyes quiet in her narrow face, not like the shiny, dark stars in the picture that had been in the den. She was another survivor of the war Dad implied we'd all lived through. It made me feel closer to her than ever.

"Why, of course you can, Glennis." She trailed her fingers along my cheek. "And Louise and the twins, too. We'll learn how to be a family again. Of course, it won't be the same, but . . ." She hesitated. "If Vinnie is getting ready for college, he probably won't want to go with us, but he can always come down to visit us on holidays. At Christmas, we'll put luminarias along our driveway, and we'll have a piñata, the way folks in New Mexico do."

I stayed the whole two hours, and had lunch with my mother in the cafeteria at Fair Haven. Everything we ate was some shade of green or orange. Lettuce, spinach, carrots, tangerines. My mother had always liked that sort of food—Nana always said it was good for a person's complexion—so I was glad she could eat a lot of it here.

When I left, she held on to me for a long while. I laid my cheek against her smooth, plain hair that till today I'd never realized was a lot like mine. The person I put my arms around was my mother—but she was someone else, too. A hostage of what was going on inside her head; someone who'd need my help pretty soon. Louise's, too. Right then and there, I decided not to waste any time letting Louise know that eventually she'd have to quit being a princess.

"Dear Louise," I wrote as soon as I got back to Wanda's, "I went to see Mom today. I think she's feeling pretty good, but you'll be surprised how she looks. Nice, but a lot different. She's thinner than she used to be, and doesn't wear eyeshadow or mascara anymore." I didn't mention anything about the pale band where her wedding ring used to be.

"The doctor says she's getting better, and she thinks she'd like to move to Albuquerque when she's all well. She wants to get the twins back, not to mention you and me. Isn't that great? Vinnie can come to visit us on his breaks from college. For a while, it'll be a house full of women! I think it'll be fun to live down there, just us women, don't you, Louise? Mom says the desert has a certain dry cleanness about it. I suppose she's right, but since you and me have never been to a desert, how would we know? I hope we can get a house made out of adobe, like you see in pictures, with a cactus garden. Mom says we'll make luminarias at Christmas, and let's you and me get some silver jewelry, with turquoise stones. Sometimes I can wear yours, and I'll let you wear mine, okay, Louise?"

I waited for my sister to answer—she was the only one in the family who liked to write letters, so I figured I wouldn't have to wait very long—but I was surprised when she called me three nights later. Wanda was at work, and I'd already put Skipper to bed.

"What you said in your letter about moving to Albuquerque," Louise began slowly. Her voice sounded confident, hardly shy at all. "Well, Glennie, I'm not sure I want to."

"Albuquerque will be fun!" I exclaimed. "Listen, I just found out every summer they have this big hot-air balloon festival down there. And Albuquerque is famous for its symphony and for all the painters and poets who live there, especially in the summer. You're absolutely going to love it, Louise," I promised.

"But it might be better for me to stay right here, where I already know everybody," Louise said. "You know how long it takes me to make friends, Glennie. Vinnie, well, Vinnie always was Mr. Personality, but I never had that knack. Now I'm the treasurer in Booster Club—and guess what? I'm assistant editor on the school paper, too."

"You just want to stay there where you can pretend you're a princess!" I yelled. "Where you can make believe you're an only child! Well, you're not, Louise! You've got three sisters, a brother, plus a mother who needs you!" When Skipper staggered out of his room, rubbing the sleep out of his eyes, I realized how loud my voice had gotten.

"Is that so awful?" my sister asked quietly. She wasn't angry, but there was no apology in her voice, either. "Is it so terrible to want to feel special? It always seemed like Vinnie came first. He was so good at everything—sports, debate club, was always president of something. Nothing I ever did seemed to get the kind of attention he got for doing the least little old thing." She paused, and when she went on there was a firmness in her voice I'd never heard before. "Anyway, Ramona and Robert are plump."

"Ramona and Robert are *what?*" I screeched.

"Momma was always thin—you were, too, thin as a

pin—plus, you were always so easy to get along with, Glennie. Vinnie was a charmer, and the twins were so cute, everybody wanted to squeeze them to death. All *I* ever was was pudgy and shy.''

''Mom told you that was only baby fat!'' I reminded my sister through clenched teeth. Anyway, I personally never thought of my sister as actually fat. She was more like one of those girls in those paintings by what's-his-name—Rubens?—just round and soft and rosy-cheeked. She was just making excuses, so I started to tell her stuff I remembered from art appreciation class about Rubens and how girls that looked like the ones in his paintings were real popular once upon a time. Only she wouldn't let me finish.

''I'm not being as selfish as you seem to think, Glennie. You don't know how happy Ramona and Robert are with me here. Okay, so they make me feel special—but that's the way I make them feel, too.''

My quiet sister—the one Dad said was shyer even than me—had found something, and all of a sudden I knew exactly what it was. She'd found a new place for herself, one that fit her. So I had to wonder: What about you, Glennis Margaret Reilly? Where do *you* fit?

After library period, I ran up behind Mary and Karalyn in the hall. Overnight, I decided not to waste any more time before making a new life. If Louise, plump and even shyer than me, had done it, I could, too.

''Listen, my aunt isn't working Saturdays anymore, so if you guys are still having sleepovers—'' They both looked at me suspiciously.

''I really wanted to go last time,'' I explained, ''but like I said, Skipper's only seven. He sees spooks in every corner. You know how little kids are.'' They gave each other secret looks, the kind friends exchange, the same ones I used to trade with Dee and Renae.

"Actually, we are," Karalyn said. "We just figured you didn't like us or something. You act, well, sort of stuck-up sometimes. Like you're better'n anybody else." I suppose that was how it had seemed to them. Karalyn conferred briefly with Mary, then said, "Can you come over to Mary's house on Friday? Then in the morning we'll all go out to the mall. There's going to be a Beads and Bangles fair, and we can load up on a ton of junk jewelry, okay?"

It would be almost like my old life. Except that it would be a new one. That's what Vinnie had now. Louise, too. Even my mother, who wore a pale band on her finger instead of a ring, and dreamed of a different life in the New Mexico desert.

❧ Chapter Ten

When I first moved to Burnsville, I was a lot like Dorothy in *The Wizard of Oz.* I was looking for a yellow brick road, too. I didn't want to go to Kansas, of course; I wanted to go home to Kenwood. After finding out about my dad, though, then hearing my mother say she'd like to live in Albuquerque, it was pretty plain that wasn't ever going to happen.

So beginning right after I visited Fair Haven, whenever I caught myself thinking about my old life, I gave myself a hard mental pinch. Which made it seem natural—when I noticed the announcement on the bulletin board outside the school administration office about signing up for the spring session of peewee wrestling—to stop and read what it said.

FOR BOTH BOYS AND GIRLS, I read, which made my eyes pop. What would Skipper say when he found out girls wrestled, too? SIGN-UP DEADLINE: WEDNESDAY, 12 NOON. PLEASE REPORT TO THE GYM ON SATURDAY, 9 A.M., TO MEET COACHES AND OBTAIN INFORMATION REGARDING NECESSARY UNIFORMS AND EQUIPMENT.

Wednesday noon. That was today. I looked at my

watch. I had five minutes. I went in and put my cousin's name on the sign-up sheet. Helping Skipper get socialized would be one of my projects as I built a new life for myself. I would do what Louise did, even if it killed me.

Alas, the object of my good intentions turned an extra shade of pale when, just before bedtime, I mentioned the big favor I'd done him as we ate graham crackers dunked in milk.

"No way," Skipper declared flatly. "Wrestling's for guys like Buster Wallace. Guys who like to sweat."

"There's nothing wrong with sweat, Skipper. The best people do it. Just think, Arnold Schwarzenegger got rich and famous on sweat. And guess what?"

My cousin refused to look at me. "For every meet you attend, you get a ribbon. No kidding, Skipper—just for showing up! That's to help kids like you who are sort of nervous about sports. It's to build up your confidence and self-esteem."

"Esteem, schmeem," he snorted, then a crafty look lighted his eyes. "What kind of ribbon?" he demanded.

"Well, it's small," I admitted, "but it's got this dangly little gold gizmo on it, sort of like a medallion. And I saw a picture of some of the trophies they give out if you win first or second or third place in a match. The statue of a kid set on a plastic base. Whole thing looks like it's made of real gold. Pretty impressive." I rolled my eyes to encourage him.

Skipper dunked another graham cracker in his milk, then nibbled on the softened edge. "Wouldn't my dad be proud?" he murmured wistfully.

For some reason, I never thought about Skipper actually having a dad. Mostly because I couldn't remember much about Roman Wayfield, who, according to stories

I wasn't supposed to have heard, left home after a big fight with Wanda when Skipper was only three years old. Skipper's eyes got a misty look in them and turned pink at the rims, making him look like a sad rabbit.

"I don't get to see my dad since he moved away to Florida," he said. "He promised he'd come back to visit me. He did, too. Once. Then the next time he called and said he couldn't make it. His car broke down, he didn't have enough money for a plane ticket. I remember he had big muscles, though." Skipper carved a shape in the air the size of an elephant's leg. Then he laid his cracker on the table with a *thonk* and mooshed it around, leaving a disgusting brown trail across the plastic cloth.

"People shouldn't have kids if they don't ever want to see 'em!" he muttered fiercely. I'd never seen Skipper get truly mad before, but I figured if he could get worked up enough to zero in on his dad like that, then maybe he'd do okay in wrestling.

"Even girls wrestle," I said, trying to clinch the deal.

"So?" He leaned over and licked up the graham cracker road he'd made. "Let 'em wrestle till their brains look like this." He shot me a black scowl, and deliberately made a fresh brown mess on the tablecloth.

I could see I was getting nowhere, so it seemed best to let the subject rest for a couple days. Instead of hassling him, I practiced my speech about swans on him until bedtime. It wasn't the first time I'd used Skipper for an audience, but he always listened as if everything I said was something he'd never heard before. Then I helped him get his teeth brushed before he got into his pj's.

Before he went to sleep, Skipper climbed up the stairs

to say good night again. He stayed so long, I realized he had something more important on his mind.

"Even girls wrestle?"

"The sign-up sheet said they could if they wanted to." I yawned casually, as if I'd put the idea of wrestling totally out of my mind.

"But Mom always likes to sleep in on Saturday morning," he whined. "It'll make her mad to have to get up early and help me get ready. And for sure somebody's gotta go with me. At least in the beginning. Till I get some of that esteem stuff."

"No problem. I'll go with you."

Good grief! What had I done? I'd just blown my chance to go to the mall! A crazy wish that Skipper would suddenly chicken out darted through my mind.

He crawled up on the end of my bed. "You will?" His hair, like Wanda's, wouldn't lay down smooth; it stuck up in wispy spears, too. He tugged on one of them. Next, he gnawed on a knuckle. Lastly, he adjusted the crotch of his pajamas.

"Okay," he said finally. "If you take me, I'll go once. Just to see what it's like." Which meant now I'd have to tell Mary and Karalyn and their bunch that I couldn't go to the sleepover after all. I wouldn't have a chance to buy junk at the Beads and Bangles fair. They'd probably never give me another chance to get into their group, either. I'd just become an assistant wrestling coach; my own social life would have to be put on hold, probably for keeps.

When we got home after the introductory wrestling session on Saturday, Wanda groaned out loud when we showed her the list of what Skipper needed.

"All this? Just to wrestle?" She pronounced *wrestle*

as if it were spelled *wrassle*. She read off each item and got crabbier with each one.

"Special shoes. A head guard with a chin protector. Knee pads. A sport bag to put it all in. Entrance fees for every match. Not cheap, I can see that!" It was plain she wished she'd been consulted first.

"It will do him good," I pointed out when Skipper was out of earshot. "He doesn't get enough exercise, Wanda. It will be better for him than sitting in front of the tube every Saturday. At home, the twins had dancing lessons on Saturday morning. I went to riding class, Louise had piano, and Vinnie was always doing some sport."

Wanda raised her eyebrows. "And may I remind you, kiddo, that once upon a time you also had somebody who could foot the bill for everything?" I wondered what Wanda would think if I told her it had been paid for with money stolen from widows and orphans.

The next Saturday, Skipper looked terribly scrawny in his wrestling outfit, which was a skintight, sleeveless, one-piece pea green suit called a singlet. There was a big yellow *E,* for Edison Elementary, on his bony little chest. His skin was as white and transparent-looking as those long, pale gizmos that grow out of a potato that's been kept in a pantry too long.

He took one look at himself in the hall mirror, hated what he saw, and refused to go to the second session.

"Listen, Skipper, every time a person tries something new, it's always scary. It takes courage. A person has to be brave." I kept my voice low so as not to disturb Wanda.

He stared daggers at me. "I don't have courage and I'm not brave," he hissed. "I'm a sissy. Lots of people say so. Even my dad did once, so it must be true. That's how come I got the nickname Skipper. It's a weenie name. Everybody knows I don't fit a name like Roman!''

"Lighten up, Skipper," I soothed. "Give yourself a break." I watched as he peeled off his singlet. It took him less than half a minute to strip down to his bare skin. I had wrecked my chance to sleep over at Mary's house for the privilege of seeing a seven-year-old kid stand stark naked before me, covered with goose bumps the size of grapes.

"Listen, Skipper, I'll buy you something if you'll just go one more time." After all, Wanda had already invested a bundle in all his wrestling gear.

Skipper's eyes narrowed. "That's bribery." He shivered, and covered strategic parts of his anatomy with crossed palms as he considered what he could wring out of me. "How about a pet?" he asked, his teeth chattering.

"Your mom definitely wouldn't be crazy about that, Skipper." I held the singlet out to him. "Anyway, you guys already have Sugar. You don't need another pet."

"I mean one of my own," he insisted. He probably wanted a dog. Most kids do. Once, I did. But it wouldn't be fair; Sugar was just too old to put up with a puppy. The minute you brought it into the house—noisy, with its cheerful, beady little eyes and toenails that clicked wickedly along the floor—well, the poor old girl would have a heart attack and die on the spot.

"You know what I've always wanted?" Skipper's teeth chattered harder. I waited, because it was plain he intended to tell me. "A bird. One that sings."

"You mean a parakeet?"

"A blue one. A kid brought his to show-and-tell once.

It had a cage with silver bars, and the teacher put it on the corner of her desk. It sang all day. It made the prettiest sound. It was Kenny Osweiler who bought it." A pinched, jealous look came into my cousin's pale eyes. "Kenny thought he was so smart, having his own bird and all."

"All right, Skipper." Just the same, there was something he had to understand. "Now this isn't a bribe, so don't get the wrong idea. What I'll do is, I'll make you this deal, okay? We'll do sort of a trade. You go to wrestling this morning, and in exchange I'll get you a bird of your choice."

"A blue one?"

I nodded. He started to put his singlet on. "But you can't take it back to the store if I decide I hate wrestling and never go again, okay?" I nodded, and sent up a little prayer that wrestling would turn out to be something he could live with.

"Wrestling, like other sports, isn't merely a physical exercise," the coach, Mr. Armstrong, told all the kids. Mats were positioned on the floor of the gym, and I sat in the bleachers with brothers and sisters and parents, who, since it was so early in the morning, could hardly keep their eyes open.

"As in any sport, some of the most important lessons are philosophical." I saw Skipper's brows draw together when Mr. Armstrong used that word *philosophical*.

"Wrestling is not about winning or losing," the coach went on, a short man with muscles out to there. "It's about good sportsmanship. The one-on-one nature of wrestling offers boys and girls a chance to develop personal confidence and self-reliance."

Skipper listened carefully. I did, too, since I was the

one who was responsible for him being here. "In this sport, a player doesn't need a ball, a bat, or a racket," said the coach. "The implement used in wrestling is the wrestler's own body." Skipper shuddered, and looked down at his own skinny white one.

Then all the kids practiced stretching exercises and how to maintain the correct positions on the mat. First the bottom position, then the top, and how to hold what Mr. Armstrong called "a shell." When they were all done, Skipper was sweaty, but he looked sort of happy, too.

At the pet store, Skipper looked at every single bird in the place before he finally decided which one he wanted. "The yellow ones are pretty," he admitted. "Sort of like dandelions with legs. But Kenny Osweiler had a blue one, and that's the color I want, too."

I was going to give him a lecture about envy, but decided that could come later. The cage we bought had a water cup and a seed dish that hooked onto the bars and were removable. We also got a cuttlebone, a swing, and a mirror, so the bird could entertain itself when none of us was around. I was using my own money, and could afford to be generous now that I knew I'd never have to buy a plane ticket to someplace like New York or San Francisco to get secret documents out of any locker.

"So what do you want to name him?" I asked Skipper as we walked home. It was a mild day, so I didn't worry too much about the bird getting a chill. Skipper carried the bird food and the toys, and I steadied the cage I carried between us.

"I can't think of any good ones," he complained. He

pulled on a tuft of hair. "Lemme see. Sugar is named Sugar—so maybe we ought to call him Salt!"

"That's a real dumb name, Skipper. Anyway, salt is white, and your bird is blue."

"We'll call him Blue, then!"

"Sheesh. What an imagination. Anyone can see the bird is blue," I said. I thought of the fairy tale about the bluebird of happiness, but since we weren't exactly a storybook sort of family, it didn't seem smart to call him Happy. Then I thought about Alice and the wonderland she discovered after she fell down the rabbit hole, about Lewis Carroll who envisioned all the adventures she would have, most of them filled with perilous surprises. Our lives—Skipper's and mine—were more like that.

"Let's call him Lewis, Skipper."

"Lewis?" Skipper peered hard at the cage. "Lewis," he said again, as if the name pleased him. The cage was wrapped with paper, and I thought I heard the bird murmur to itself when we said its name.

"A bird!" Wanda screeched when we walked in the back door. "I sure wish you'd asked first if this was an okay idea!" Once she started, she kept right on yelling. "Glen, I have to say that you just haul off and do stuff without giving a single thought to how things will turn out! First it's wrassling, now it's birds. You remind me a lot of Nana Reilly, you know that? Always tinkering in people's lives, adjusting them to suit yourself. Now just what d'you suppose Sugar is going to think about all this?" she demanded, her hands on her hips.

"It was the only way I could get Skipper to go to his first class this morning," I whispered behind my hand.

"How'd he do?" she asked, lowering her voice as Skipper carried the bird into the living room.

"Great," I reported. "Today was mostly stretching exercises, but next week the kids will be matched with someone the same size they are, so it's really fair. Skipper'll do okay, once he gets the knack of it."

Skipper found a good place for the bird—on top of the TV. "If he listens to shows every day, he might even learn how to talk, just like a parrot," he speculated. Sugar came into the living room to find out what all the excitement was about. I thought she smiled at Lewis. But I guess she realized her birding days were over, if she'd ever had any in the first place, because she never once got up on the TV to get a better look at him.

That night, Skipper trekked up the stairs again to say good night to me for a second time. He crawled up on the bed, and I put my math homework aside. It was plain he had something more to say.

"You're practically like a sister or something," he began.

"You already told me that, Skipper."

"I mean, a sister would do something really nice, like bribe me with a bird."

"I didn't bribe you, Skipper," I reminded him. "We made a deal, remember?"

Skipper stretched out at the foot of the bed. I hoped he didn't intend to stay all night. "Well, anyway, thanks for Lewis. I really like him." Then before I could say, "You're welcome," he was off the bed and down the stairs, as if he was nervous about being so agreeable. Actually, if he'd wanted to stay all night, I would've let him. To think one little bird could've made him so happy. It made me think about birds in general. Like pigeons, for instance. Swans, even.

Naturally, that made me think of Cooper Davis, who knew things about both. I kind of missed seeing him—

but till peewee wrestling was over, I couldn't catch the bus to the FDC in hopes of seeing him at the park.

I snapped off the light on Wanda's rickety bedside table. I smiled to myself in the dark. So maybe I'd just have to stop by the Burger Bonanza someday after school. Like tomorrow.

I pretended I just wanted a frosty malt. I sat at the counter and watched the swinging doors that led into the kitchen. When a mom and dad and two kids got up from their table, leaving dirty plates behind, I figured Cooper would show up pretty soon. He did, and after he'd picked everything up, I gave him a feeble little, "Hi, Cooper."

"Glennis!" he said, and actually seemed glad to see me. "I was beginning to think you'd left town."

"Every Saturday I have to take my cousin Skipper to peewee wrestling," I explained, "so I can't go out to the prison like I used to."

Cooper leaned one hip against the stool next to mine. He smiled, and I thought if I was older I might like him the way Louise liked Whit Anderson when she was in ninth grade and waited patiently every night for the phone to ring, which it never did. Whit decided he liked Sallyjo Hansen, who was so skinny she hardly cast a shadow, which naturally made Louise feel worse than ever.

"You ever make it up with your dad?" Cooper asked.

I shook my head. "Not yet." I didn't mention maybe I'd never go to the prison again. But if he could ask personal questions, I didn't see any reason why I couldn't, too. "So, you written any new poems lately?"

He gave me one of his strange, wolf-eyed looks. "Yeah, actually I have." He smiled; whenever he did, it made him look like a different person from the one I thought I knew. "It's about you," he said.

"Me?" I wasn't the sort of person anyone would write a poem about, so I wondered what he could've put in it. "You going to let me read it?"

"Maybe later, when I get all the words right."

"The guys my brother Vinnie used to run around with wouldn't have been caught dead writing poems. So how come you do?"

"I didn't, not till I got stuck in PORT," Cooper admitted. "We go to school there, too, you know." He settled himself on the stool as if he intended to have a long conversation.

"It's one of those alternative schools, the kind for kids who don't fit in anywhere else. The guy who teaches us English showed us some of his stuff one day. It was kind of weird. I mean, I used to think only ladies who wore white dresses and stayed in their rooms all day wrote poetry. But Mr. Inman said it was a good way to get in touch with yourself, which is one of the things we're supposed to learn how to do while we're there. You know, so we don't screw up the minute we get out. He told us the world starts to look different if you can get to know yourself better."

I saw the manager of the Burger Bonanza shoot a frowny look in Cooper's direction, so I slid off my stool and got ready to leave. "I gotta go," I said. "I'll see you around."

"Hang in there, kid," he said right back. "It's gonna be all right." I hurried out and headed for Wanda's. It killed me when people were sympathetic, because it still made me feel like crying. After Rags, I hadn't cried anymore; I wasn't about to start now.

🌺 Chapter Eleven

*E*very Thursday after school, Skipper and I had to clean the living room.

"If you guys do it during the week, it'll mean we won't have to spend our whole weekends doing boring stuff like housework," Wanda explained. "Then we can take time out for a movie or go shopping. You know, do something together that's fun." I didn't mind; I figured the experience would come in handy when I started to help Mom keep house after she, Louise, and the twins and I finally got settled in our adobe house in Albuquerque.

"What's in all these stupid boxes?" Skipper grumbled, because it was his turn to vacuum around the ones Wanda had moved down from my bedroom and stuffed into a corner next to the TV. He rammed the vacuum against them as if it were a bulldozer and he intended to excavate a tunnel into the next room. The horrible racket scared poor Lewis, who ricocheted back and forth off the bars of his cage.

"Take it easy, Skipper, you're gonna give Lewis a seizure," I warned. "Those boxes are full of scraps your mom's been saving."

"Scraps of what?"

"Fabric. Once, your mom sewed her own clothes, just like mine did." Mom had told me about the second-hand Singer machine she and Wanda got to make outfits for themselves after they learned how to sew in eighth-grade home ec. It saved money, she said, but my grand-mother Reilly despised anything that looked homemade. She said that word as if it were the disgusting kind with only four letters, causing a funny, bruised look to cross my mother's face.

"I want to see," Skipper said, and shut off the vacuum.

"Listen, Skipper, quit trying to figure out ways to weasel out of doing your fair share," I complained. "It's your turn to vacuum today. There's nothing in those boxes that would interest you. It's girl-type stuff."

He paid no attention to me, and proceeded to drag one of them into the middle of the room. Inside were pieces of material that looked older than I was. Some of the fabric had never been used at all, while most of it was odds and ends.

"Okay, you've seen 'em, now put 'em back," I ordered. But what I'd seen in those boxes gave me a brand-new idea.

On Friday, Wanda lay down on the sofa in the living room as soon as she got home from the Sup-R-Chef. "What a week," she groaned, and pressed her hand against her forehead as if it ached. I told her I'd make sloppy joes for supper, but she was so pooped she only nodded and waved me away. I used paper plates so we wouldn't have a lot of dishes to do, and after supper when we all went back out to the living room, I told Wanda about my idea.

"I don't think you ought to throw those boxes of scraps away," I said. I waited to see if she was paying attention, but she only groaned and kept her eyes closed. "I think what we should do is make a quilt, Wanda, just like you always wanted. We can all work on it together, you and me and Skipper."

Skipper perked right up when he heard his name linked with his favorite word, *together*. Wanda opened one eye, and I pointed at the boxes in the corner.

She propped herself up on one elbow. Her bleached hair was frizzy, and her complexion took on a greenish yellow glow from the light coming off the TV, which made her look seriously sick.

"A quilt?" she repeated. "Oh, Glen, I haven't thought about that project for a million years. I don't believe I want to think about it now, either." She flopped back down. "What'd I tell you about tinkering with other people's lives? So quit already. I'm almost too tired to live, much less take up a hobby."

Skipper obligingly dragged one of the boxes into the middle of the room. "But look, Mom," he urged, and held up some material with squirrels and rabbits on it. Wanda peered at it, terminally jaundiced in the glare of the TV. She roused herself enough to look vaguely interested.

"That's from an outfit I made for you when you were a baby, Skipper. You can't believe what a cute little guy you were." She smiled tenderly at him. "Sort of like a sweet little squirrel yourself." Skipper looked pleased to hear he'd been a baby once, even if he looked like a squirrel, and that his mother had made something special just for him.

Wanda mustered enough energy to reach over and lift up some fabric with blue flowers on it. "And this is from a dress I made once when I wasn't much older than you, Glen." She gave me a glance that was partly sociable and partly you-and-your-dumb-ideas. "Your mother made one just like it with yellow flowers on it." Her face softened, and all of a sudden she didn't seem so tired.

I took that as a good sign. "Well, guess what, Wanda? The other day I got this book about quilts from the school library." I'd come across it when I was supposed to be looking for one about swans. I grabbed my book bag and dug it out. "Listen up, you guys. I'll read off the names of some of these famous old colonial quilt patterns, okay? I swear some of these names are as neat as how the quilts look when they're done." I checked to see if they were listening. Skipper was; I couldn't tell about Wanda.

"Buggy Wheel. Log Cabin. Bear's Paw. Flying Geese. Jacob's Ladder. Now do those sound great, or what? It says here that's how people preserved their history back in the old days. A quilt was sort of like a scrapbook, and did double duty by keeping people warm at night."

Wanda sat up, and Skipper came to sit beside me on the couch. We all looked closer at the pictures. In one of them, the spokes on the Buggy Wheel were sharpened to star points, and the hubs were bright green. "I like that one," Skipper declared. The pad of the Bear's Paw was brown, and the four toes seemed to have long claws on their tips. Flying Geese showed blue and purple geese winging across a pale gray sky, and the Jacob's

Ladder of blue and yellow seemed to reach straight up to heaven.

"Let's, Mom!" Skipper exclaimed. "Let's us make a quilt!"

"Oh, it's way too much work," Wanda murmured, and let her glance drift back to the TV.

"We could cut the pieces out together," I suggested. "Not everything at once, just a few every night." Now Wanda looked sicker than before. I could see the job sounded way too humongous to her. "Okay, so let's go for a wall hanging instead of a quilt," I said. "It'd be smaller and easier for us to finish. After we get it done we might try something bigger. Look, there's even graph paper in the book that shows you how to measure, and how to count how many pieces of everything you need."

"Ah, c'mon, Mom!" Skipper whined, and practiced his sad rabbit look on her.

Wanda toyed with her hair as she listened, which made it frizzier than ever. I'd already decided that I would make a pillow cover for each of the twins, Flying Geese for Allie, and a Wagon Wheel for Missy.

If I ever made one for myself, which would it be? What about Jacob's Ladder, which might lead me back to heaven? The truth was, even though I'd vowed to build a new life and was making myself crazy inventing new projects, every once in a while I'd get this funny little tingle, thinking *what if, what if* somehow I could get the old one back again. Isn't it funny how people don't want to give up their favorite dream, even when the dream is all worn out, even when they know deep down it can't ever come true?

"But only a few pieces every night," Wanda agreed finally. "I'm just too tired when I come home to spend much time on anything as picky as quilting,'' she added, punctuating her agreement with another frown in my direction.

That's not how it turned out, though. We finally voted on which pattern we wanted to tackle, and Buggy Wheel won by a vote of two to one (Skipper wanted the Bear Paw). Once Wanda got started the next night, she worked even after Skipper and I went to bed. Pretty soon all the pieces were cut and we were ready to start sewing them together. We read the instructions, and used the same teeny-weeny stitches that were illustrated in the book.

Skipper couldn't handle a needle too well, so mostly he watched Wanda and me while we sewed. The TV was turned off, and Wanda kept the radio low. As we worked, sometimes Skipper sang songs from school—"Itsy-Bitsy Spider'' was his favorite—or Wanda hummed a country-western tune about love gone wrong.

I should have felt happy and contented. We were cozy. Supper had been good; the dishes were done. Sugar was asleep in her basket; Lewis murmured under the towel that covered his cage after sundown.

I was practically killing myself trying to do what Louise had done, so how come it wasn't working? My sister had joined the Booster Club and was on the school paper—and hadn't I invented all kinds of projects for my new life, too? But there was still an ache under my heart. What I wanted wasn't something new; it was everything I'd lost. When you feel like that, you can't really be happy. You're still waiting for everything to go back to the way it was before.

I met Skipper at the corner and walked home with him. He'd gotten a star in his arithmetic workbook, which he'd peeled off and stuck in the middle of his forehead. "I wonder if Mom will notice," he said.

As we rounded the corner only half a block from home, a dog came loping down the street toward us. I realized it must be the one I heard barking that evening when Skipper and I walked home from the playground at Gibson. A man with white hair, flustered and breathless, followed him. "Grab his collar!" he cried, waving a leash at us at the same time. "He got out of the yard accidentally and now he won't come back!"

The dog bounded forward gleefully, as if he'd been waiting all day just for the sight of Skipper and me. "Here, boy," I called, like I used to call to Rags after school. With his tongue lolling out of his mouth, his eyes merry, the old man's dog came right up to me like Rags once did. His collar was blue leather and I hooked my fingers under it.

"I got him, mister," I called to the old man, who huffed up the street in his slippers, a frayed red sweater hanging off his shoulders like a ratty old Superman cape.

"Oh, what a relief!" he said. "He's not a bad dog, it's just that he's too big for our small yard. Used to exercise him every day, but he needs more now than I can give him." He tapped his chest. "My heart, you know. Six months ago I had bypass surgery, and it's taken me a while to get back on my feet."

The dog wasn't as beautiful as Rags, but was friendly and nearly wagged his back end off as I handed him over to the old man, who clipped the leash onto the dog's collar. To my surprise, he passed the leash back to me.

"Could you just hang on to him for a minute, young lady, while I catch my breath?"

Together, the four of us walked down the street toward home. It turned out that the old man lived in the yellow house on the corner, a place that needed paint almost as bad as Wanda's. It was plain to see the yard behind it wasn't big enough for a dog the size of the one that gamboled in front of us.

"I used to walk him around the block three times a day," the old man said. "But now, well, I just can't do as much as I used to."

When we got to his end of the block, I passed the leash back to him. "I had a dog once," I said. "If you want, I'll walk yours whenever I have time." I didn't mention that Rags was much more beautiful, and had a disposition a saint would die for.

"I'm sure Prince would enjoy that," the old man said. "By the way, I'm Mr. Byerly. I know the lad— his mother is that pretty young Mrs. Wayfield who wears such lively outfits. But you—" He squinted at me uncertainly.

"I'm Glennis, Skipper's cousin, and I'm staying here a while," I said. I didn't mention my last name for fear he'd recognize it from all the stuff that had been in the newspapers and on TV a year ago.

"I can't pay you much," Mr. Byerly said apologetically.

"Oh, I'll do it just for the fun of it," I said. In a way it would be, even though it was Rags who deserved to be called a prince, and Mr. Byerly's dog looked like a rag.

It look me a long time to get to sleep that night. Too much had been happening lately. Skipper had almost pinned his opponent in peewee wrestling; Lewis sang sometimes, though not often enough to suit Skipper; our wall hanging was almost finished; now I was on the hook to walk somebody's dog once a day.

Suddenly, I needed to talk to someone. Bad. Someone who'd been part of my life before. I looked at the clock. It was only nine thirty. I tiptoed downstairs and dialed my uncle Roger's house. I had temporarily given up on Louise, who was so busy with all her clubs that she hardly even wrote anymore, only short letters that were mostly examples of how popular she was now. I hoped my aunt would answer. She did.

"So how are Allie and Missy?" I asked. "I know they're too little to write letters yet, but I think about them every day."

"They're doing just great," my aunt assured me. Her voice was warm, like an aunt's is supposed to be. "Oh, it was hard for them at first," she confessed. "As you know, Derek and Jason can be quite a handful. But the girls have started to take tennis lessons, and seem to be enjoying them a lot." I couldn't imagine our mild and dainty twins playing anything as athletic as tennis.

"And how are *you*, Glennis?" Aunt Helen asked. It was the question I didn't want anyone to ask because I was afraid I'd be tempted to answer it.

"Well . . ." I began, but couldn't go on.

"I know it must be tough, Glennis," my aunt said softly. She has a round face, freckles, a smile as wide as the Nile, and I could see her plainly in my mind's eye. Aunt Helen was healthy and ordinary and would never give a thought to fussing about whether or not she wore a color called taupe. "With time, it'll get easier, Glennis," she promised me.

It was practically the same thing Cooper had said. Everybody seemed to know something I didn't. Only something was still wrong, and after my aunt hung up, the ache under my heart felt worse than ever.

I went back upstairs and crawled into bed. I pulled

the covers up to my chin and stared into the darkness. I knew why I felt so awful. Why all my projects and ideas weren't working. Because I couldn't forgive the person who'd wrecked everything. No way could I ever forgive John Reilly for what he'd done to all of us. Not ever.

Well, then, maybe what I needed was a bigger, better project. Not another little one that Wanda and Skipper and I did together. A big one, that would bring the rest of the family all back together again.

🌸 *Chapter Twelve*

"**Y**ou know what, Wanda?" I asked as we walked home from Skipper's third wrestling match. This time, he'd pinned his opponent, fair and square, and now he swaggered ahead of us with Buster Wallace, who all of a sudden was his best buddy.

"I've got another great idea, Wanda. You want to hear it?" I didn't see how she could object. After all, our wall hanging had turned out great. We'd put it up over the sofa, where it really brightened up the room, not to mention that since Skipper was getting regular exercise, a pink glow often showed on his pale cheeks. She had to admit it: All my ideas worked out really well.

Wanda exhaled noisily. She pushed her bangs out of her eyes. She limped a little because she said one of her cowboy boots was squeezing her big toe. "You want the honest-to-god truth, Glen? No. I definitely do not want to hear about any more of your ideas. You've got altogether too many to suit me." She spoke about them as if they were termites, as if she needed to make a note to call the pest control man.

"One thing I've noticed about these schemes you concoct," my aunt went on. Her voice was pinched and cranky, like her toe probably felt. "They end up being a ton of work for a certain already-overworked waitress. Just look at what's happened to my life since you moved in with Skipper and me." I knew she was going to itemize her complaints whether I wanted to hear them or not.

"Listen up here, Glen. Soon as you mentioned my poor little guy looked like a piece of cheese, I've been trying to cook better. Right?" I nodded. "I was up late every night till we finished that crazy wall hanging. Right?" I nodded. "Not to mention sometimes I have to clean a certain bird's cage when I get home from work. You get my drift?"

"I'm mostly the one who takes care of Lewis," I objected. She only had to clean his cage once, because somehow he dumped over his water dish when I was busy with my homework and didn't notice right away. Part of what she said was true, though, even if at first she was so out of practice with cooking that a few of our suppers were pretty weird. That peanut butter-flavored french toast with maple syrup had been a disaster. Lately, though, I had to admit the stuff she cooked was really tasty.

The sun was warm on our shoulders, which made my new topic seem appropriate. I ignored the fact Wanda had just told me she didn't want to hear about any more of my plans. She'd like this one, if she just gave herself a chance to think about it.

"Remember those family picnics we had every Memorial Day when my folks lived on Stone Barn Road?"

Wanda smiled, and didn't answer right away. She seemed to be running a videotape through her mind about what those get-togethers had been like.

"Well, now, weren't they something else?" she said, and shook her head with admiration. She didn't sound as crabby anymore. "Your mom and dad really knew how to entertain, didn't they? Everyone had such a great time, and for some of us it was the only chance we got to see each other from one year to the next."

Dad always rented a big tent for the occasion, one with yellow-and-white stripes. He hired a man to roast a whole pig over a cherrywood fire. A catering service made mountains of potato salad and two or three chocolate cakes. There were big metal tubs filled with ice to chill as many cans of pop as we could drink. A badminton net was put up, plus hoops for croquet; there were dartboards, too, and at the end of the yard a special place for playing horseshoes. All the relatives sat around talking about the picnics from other years. A couple years ago Dad got a camcorder so we could make videos of ourselves.

"This will be the first time I can remember that there won't be a picnic," I said. We walked in silence for another half a block. "So what I was thinking, Wanda, well, maybe we should be the ones to have the picnic this year."

My aunt stopped in the middle of the sidewalk and turned to me, her mouth open with astonishment. "*We?* Excuse me? Turn that *w* upside down, my girl, and you get *me!* Didn't I just explain myself to you, Glen? Not only am I making quilts, getting up early on Saturday morning to watch my kid wrassle, cooking my brains out—now you want me to start throwing parties, too?"

"I'll help you," I said. "And I'll help pay, too."

I'd become just like Nana: Money was my solution for everything. My stash of cash was building up again after I'd laid out more than sixty dollars for Lewis and his cage. Sharing expenses with Wanda wouldn't be a problem at all.

"Skipper and I will make the invitations ourselves, so you won't have any charges for calls on your phone bill, okay? The picnic won't have to be as fancy as Dad's. We'll just charcoal some hot dogs instead of trying to roast a whole pig. Maybe you could make some potato salad." Wanda grimaced at the idea. "And Skipper and I will bake a bunch of cupcakes out of some packaged mix. Some chocolate, some white, with those little colored crinkles on the frosting. So what d'you say, Wanda?"

"In case it has escaped your attention, Glen, my backyard is the size of a postage stamp," Wanda pointed out. She'd gone back to being crabby again. "This address isn't Stone Barn Road, in case you haven't noticed, where you guys had an acre of space, lots of lawn and trees, a creek with its own little bridge, nice stuff like that. I don't have to hire anyone to cut *my* grass. I could trim it with fingernail clippers and be done real quick."

"Hey, that just means there won't be much cleanup afterward, Wanda!" I exclaimed. "Means we won't have to rent a tent, either."

"You think of everything, Glen," Wanda said, and gave me a frown. I didn't say so, but sometimes that was true. Everything included the fact that of course there'd be one person who wouldn't be invited. John Reilly, who was only two miles away at the FDC.

After lunch, Skipper and I went straight to the mall

to buy some construction paper, pens, and glue. I checked the calendar to see when Memorial Day fell.

"It's always on the last Monday in May," Wanda said, as if she'd already accepted the fact we were about to become party-givers. A three-day weekend meant there'd be no problem with everyone driving down to Burnsville. Since there wasn't enough room for everyone to sleep over at her place, Wanda suggested I ought to enclose a list of handy motels in the area. I figured maybe Louise could stay upstairs with me, though, and we could talk when the lights were out like we did back and forth across the hall when we lived together.

"What shape should these invitations be?" Skipper wanted to know. "Square, like little boxes? Or hey, how about like they were balloons? A balloon's just a circle, and would be super-easy to make." He folded a chunk of scrap paper in half and cut a half-circle; opened up, it didn't look too bad.

"Or how about a shape like a tent?" I drew an example on a piece of paper. It was an easy shape, too, and also could be folded in half. "It would remind people of how much fun it was to come to the family picnics we used to have." With a yellow Hi-Liter we even put stripes on the tents. Inside, we wrote:

> *It's been a while*
> *Since we've seen your smile,*
> *So join us on Memorial Day*
> *For lots of fun, food, and play.*

"That's awfully corny," Wanda observed, but Skipper liked the way it sounded. In the corner under the verse, I wrote RSVP.

"What's that mean?" Skipper wanted to know.

"It's French," I told him. "*Repondez, s'il vous plaît,* which means 'please answer our invitation.' " When the cards were finished, each of us signed our names under the rhyme. Skipper's eyes were sparkly.

"Me and Mom never had this much company before. This time, it'll be Allie and Missy coming to *my* picnic, not me going to theirs!"

Apparently not everyone understood French, because it seemed to take a long time for the responses to start rolling in. It was almost ten days before the first acceptance came from Louise. She included a P.S. on the bottom of a note to me, telling me she'd been invited to the senior prom.

"You know who asked me, Glennie?" she went on. "Whit Anderson, that's who!" I knew she must be as happy now as Ramona. "And I'm going to bring Ramona and Robert to the picnic, too, okay? So tell Vinnie he won't have to stop in Kenwood to pick me up. Robert and Ramona said it's just as easy to drive down and back in one day, so I won't be able to stay overnight with you. Sorry, sweetie." I got the feeling she wasn't sorry at all.

Aunt Helen's answer came in next. She actually seemed happy someone had thought of the idea. "It surely would be a shame for all of us to lose track of one another," she wrote. "You won't believe how the twins have grown! You'll hardly recognize them, Glennis." I doubted that they could have changed as much as she seemed to think; after all, I'd seen them only five months ago, just before I left home.

The note that finally came from my grandmother was on cream-colored stationery that smelled of gardenias. Her opinion was quite different from Aunt Helen's.

"I'm not sure that this is a very good idea, Glennis,"

she wrote in a dainty script that belied her iron disposition. "We have all changed and have undergone the sort of losses that mere words cannot describe. Nevertheless, you can count on your grandfather and me to put in an appearance. I presume some members of the family will try to visit your father, too."

But I didn't hear a word from my mother.

Finally, I called her at Fair Haven. "Did you get my invitation, Mom? Louise and Nana and Aunt Helen are coming, and Wanda would really like to have you come down, too. She told me you can stay with her in her room. She's got this king-size bed, so she says you won't feel crowded." On the other end of the wire, my mother gave a long, soft sigh.

"And if it's a problem for you to come alone on the bus, I'll come up so we can ride back here together. Okay?" She sighed again, but still said nothing.

"Mom?" I pressed.

"My goodness, Glennis, I never realized you were such an organizer," she murmured at last, and there was a tiny smile in her voice. The truth was, I never had to be. Before, she was the one who organized everything. For all of us. Summer camps. Pets. Clothes. Parties.

"Well, actually, Glennis, the doctor says that it would be a good idea for me to take a weekend pass now and then. Once in a while I spend an afternoon in town, so I've even had practice riding a bus. If I'm careful, and if I'm sure to not forget any of my medication, perhaps coming down to see all of you is exactly what I should do."

It was pretty plain that she counted on her pills. Did that mean there'd still be a long delay before we could get moved down to Albuquerque? I decided I'd better not mention that.

Then I did something that no matter how long I live I'll never be able to undo. Whenever I think about it, I remember what Cooper Davis told me about the swans, that they were sort of like people, with a dark side and a light side.

I found out I had a dark side, too. Really dark; black, even. Because I made out a special invitation. I colored it even more carefully than I colored any of the others, making sure the yellow stripes on the tent were just about perfect. Under the verse I wrote, "Too bad you can't join us this year." There was one stamp left over. I licked it, put it on an envelope, and addressed the invitation to John Reilly at the FDC.

❀ Chapter Thirteen

We finally got answers back to all our invitations (except the last one I'd mailed, unbeknownst to Wanda or Skipper).

We rented a bunch of stuff from the Party Place. Folding tables, stacking chairs, even an old-fashioned ice-cream freezer you had to turn with a crank. That was Wanda's idea. She said everyone would have fun helping make ice cream like in olden times, before electricity and refrigerators.

We got paper cloths decorated with red, white, and blue stars and stripes for the tables, red paper plates, blue cups, and white plastic silverware. The day before the picnic we bought fresh buns and six packages of jumbo hot dogs. Wanda said she wasn't about to make a ton of potato salad for anybody's party, not even her own, and ordered some from the deli next door to the Sup-R-Chef.

"If it rains tomorrow, I swear I will kill myself," she said, but I noticed when she looked out over the backyard she seemed happy enough to go right on living.

Okay, it wasn't as fancy as the setup in the backyard on Stone Barn Road, but it looked pretty good anyway. Skipper and I had blown up balloons and tied them to the fence posts. We got strings of patio lights in the shape of tiny Chinese lanterns and hung them from the rain troughs.

"How silly can you guys be," Wanda said. "We don't even have a patio!" I planted three red geraniums and some blue petunias in the box fastened under Wanda's kitchen window, which she admitted she'd never even noticed was there.

Two days before the picnic, a note came from Dad. I hesitated. "So open it already!" Wanda exclaimed.

"Thanks for the invitation, Glennis," I read silently, pretending it was a regular letter, not his response to an RSVP. "Well, guess what? My roommate and I—if I can call him that, considering where we both are—have come down with measles. I think we caught it from his two little boys, who were here recently for a visit. So now Dave and I are under a quarantine, can't leave our room until we're out of the infectious stage—you know, to make sure the whole institution doesn't come down with it. But please tell everyone how glad I am that all of you are getting together."

Had Dad been in the visitors' lounge, visiting with his roommate's children? Did that mean he'd been hoping his own kid might show up? The one who'd promised to be loyal, faithful, and true no matter what? I felt a moment of doubt, thinking how bad he might have felt, then my heart was closed against him again. *I'm guilty, Glennis. I did everything the prosecution said I did.* Those words would always stand between us, a mountain too high to climb over.

"What did he have to say?" Wanda wanted to know. I folded the letter in half and stuck it in the pocket of my jeans. "Nothing much," I said, and pretended not to notice the curious look she gave me.

Mom arrived the day before the party. Skipper and I went down to the bus station to meet her. She wore the dazed expression of a traveler returning from outer space.

"Hi, Aunt Mona," Skipper said, and my mother bent down on one knee to study him gravely, as if she weren't quite sure she'd ever met a human child before, even though she had five of her own.

As soon as we got back to the house, she crawled into Wanda's big bed and pulled the covers up as if the weather had suddenly turned cool. "It was a longer trip than I thought it would be," she said as I stood beside her. "Noisier. So much going on. I guess I'm not used to life on the outside." When I went in to tell her supper was ready, she was sleeping so soundly I didn't wake her up.

"Do you think she'll be all right?" I asked Wanda as we did dishes. What if my mother's breakdown had broken something inside her that nobody knew about, not even the doctors? What if she couldn't get out of bed tomorrow, wouldn't be able to return to Fair Haven when she was supposed to?

"She'll be fine," Wanda said, nudging me with her hip. "She's been through a lot. We shouldn't expect just because we're throwing a picnic that she'll automatically be her old self again. But she will be one of these days, Glen, I promise. Just you wait and see. I know my sister; she's made out of stronger stuff than you think.'' Wanda could be so practical she made me feel almost normal.

On Sunday morning I could see the sky through the slats in the new peach-colored mini-blinds Wanda finally got around to hanging in my room. The sky was perfect, almost cloudless. I opened the window a crack; I could tell it wouldn't be too hot or too cold, and there wasn't any wind. Another big plus: It was too early in the year for many mosquitoes.

Uncle Roger and his rowdy tribe were the first to show up. Naturally, I heard those savages Derek and Jason before I saw anyone else. They catapulted through the front door as if they'd been launched from Cape Canaveral. Roger clomped in behind them, a camcorder hoisted over his shoulder, filming as he came. Last through the door was Aunt Helen, along with a pair of strangers.

She hadn't mentioned on the phone that she'd cut off all the twins' long, wavy hair. ''It's just so much easier for them and me,'' she said when she noticed me staring at my sisters. The twins' hair fit their heads as snugly as two yellow bathing caps, and their noses were peeling from sunburn. They seemed taller than I remembered, and there were scabs on their knees, not to mention grime under their fingernails. They weren't precious little dolls anymore; they were just ordinary kids.

''Glennis!'' they yelled in unison. ''How about a game of tennis, Glennis?'' They doubled over, as if they'd invented that smart remark all by themselves. Then they grabbed me around the waist and tried to climb up my legs, as if they realized maybe they'd touched a raw nerve.

''Hey, you guys look so different!'' I exclaimed.

"We *are* different," Allie yelled. It was plain they were taking voice lessons from Derek and Jason.

"We don't take dancing anymore," Missy cried. "We take tennis, instead!" The word *tennis* reminded them how witty they were, and they smiled secretly at each other. "That's where we got our sunburn!" they shouted. Once, they'd been so mild and quiet; now they were almost like someone else's sisters.

"Did you guys ever get the pillow covers I sent you?"

"Yeah! They're great!" They still said things at the same time, so not everything had changed. Then they tore off to chase Skipper around the backyard, to try to trap him in a corner and tickle his ribs. He ran, but not so fast they couldn't catch him every second try.

Ramona and Robert arrived next, and Louise came up the sidewalk between them. Suddenly, I understood exactly what my sister tried to tell me on the phone. It was true: The three of them were as plump and smooth as three ripe pears hanging on a tree.

Louise reached out to me for a hug (unlike our grandmother, Louise was a great hugger), and when she wrapped me up in her soft, round arms I saw Ramona and Robert trade nervous glances. I suppose they were afraid Louise wouldn't want to leave me behind when it was time to go. That she'd want to live with Wanda, too, or else would want me to come back to Kenwood to live, ruining their perfect triangle.

They didn't need to worry, though. When Louise turned me loose, she took each of them by the hand, and instantly they were three ripe pears again. Ramona's eyes glowed with relief; Robert looked like a man who'd just won a lottery.

All the white plastic stacking chairs were arranged

around the yard, and Wanda and I started to serve lemonade right away. It wasn't long before the sound of everyone's voices drew my grandparents around the side of the house after Vinnie parked their long, dark car with its smoked windows next to the curb. My grandmother marched through the gate like a general about to review a regiment. The wings of silver hair that swept back from her brow looked as if they might actually lift her into the air.

"Yo, Glennie," Vinnie said. I was amazed to see he was growing a beard. It must have been worth about two weeks of not shaving, which made him look scruffy and a lot older. I wondered how—since he was living with Nana—he could get away with that. He bent down. "I'll tell you about it later," he whispered, as if he could read my mind. Sheesh! My brother, Vinnie, who hardly ever knew I was alive, now could read my mind?

Finally, my mother collected herself enough to come out of Wanda's bedroom. She was so pale and quiet, dressed solemnly in shades of gray, and seemed to want to cling to Wanda, who actually was younger by three years but who was the one who seemed worldly-wise now. In her new crimson shirt decorated with colorful embroidery, her black jeans and boots with run-over heels, my aunt looked like a rodeo queen who'd been on the circuit long enough to think about retiring. She'd told me herself, though, the closest she ever got to a horse was a couple times on a merry-go-round at the fair.

"How about you two fellows starting on the ice cream?" Wanda invited Roger and Robert. "Louise, you and your mother get the charcoal set up, okay?" I was happy to see my mother and my sister work so well together. My mother seemed grateful for the patient instructions Louise gave her; she smiled at my sister like an alien who was relieved to discover earthlings were kindly creatures after all. I figured it meant things would work out okay when we eventually got to New Mexico.

"More lemonade, Nana?" I suggested when I came around again with the lemonade pitcher. My grandmother allowed me to fill her glass, while my grandfather smiled agreeably and played a familiar tattoo on his knee.

"Has it worked out well for you here, Glennis?" my grandmother inquired in her crisp, unsentimental way. Her glasses had steel-blue rims, and her eyes behind them were the same color. Her profile was still as clean as one on a new coin, not the soft kind that comes to mind when you think about grandmothers.

"Yes, Nana, it really has," I told her. "It's been a chance for me to get to know Skipper a lot better, and Wanda, too," I explained. "Later, maybe you'd like to come upstairs and see how we fixed up my room. Skipper even helped me tear off the old wallpaper."

"Why, let's do it now, Glennis, while it's fresh on our minds," my grandmother suggested.

I went up behind her as we climbed the narrow stairs, and noticed how lean and strong her legs were, muscled in spite of her age, like an old marathon runner's. She inspected the peach-colored room, and—seeing it through her eyes—I noticed stuff I hadn't paid much attention to lately, like the brown spots on the ceiling, the dresser drawer that was missing a knob, the varnish peeling off the bedside table where I kept my family picture. My grandmother lowered herself carefully onto the edge of my bed.

"I brought something for you, Glennis," she announced.

"You did?" I wondered if it was taupe-colored, and if she remembered what size I wore.

She reached into her purse (it was as big as a briefcase) and took out my red ribbon from swim class, walnut frame and all. "I found it by accident as I was rearranging some boxes when we stored everything after the trial. I thought you might like to have it."

"Thanks," I said. She had seen it, and thought of me. Suddenly, I wanted to tell her that Dad had said *I'm guilty, Glennis,* but instead both of us were silent for a moment.

"I regretted to hear that your father caught the measles," she said finally. "As I recall, he never had them when he was a child. No doubt he appreciates your visits, though. Do you see him every week, as you planned?" That question made my heart hammer.

"Dad said I ought to start building a new life," I said. She nodded, and didn't take her eyes off the picture on the nightstand.

"Yes, that's what he mentioned in one of his letters to us. I think it was good advice, Glennis. Perhaps it's something we all need to do." She twisted her hands in her lap.

"Have you ever wondered why life turns out so differently from what you'd planned?" she mused, and reached for the picture. She traced the faces of each of us with the tip of her finger. My grandmother is one of those people you can admire from a distance, but it's kind of hard to like her up close. She and I had never had a truly personal conversation before, and the fact that she'd decided to have one with me now made me begin to love her a little bit.

I sat down beside her. "Sometimes I do," I admitted. "I think about how it used to be on Stone Barn Road. And sometimes I wish—" I interrupted myself. I was supposed to be looking forward, not backward.

My grandmother laid her hand on top of mine. It was light, dry, cool. The rings on her fingers were lumpy and looked expensive. "Ah, Glennis, don't make the mistake I did," she advised softly. There was a look in her eye that was almost sweet, which surprised me because I'd always thought of her as a general with a code of conduct hardly any of her troops could live up to.

"I spent a lifetime trying to make people into what they were never meant to be," she said. "And maybe that's why, in the end, your father made such a terrible mistake. . . ." Her voice trailed away, and I realized she wasn't talking to me as much as to herself. "Why, in the end, everything turned out so unlike anything I'd ever dreamed."

"It's all right, Nana," I said. How could I say any such thing? How did *I* know anything would be all right? I reached over to give her a hug. Her shoulders were square and bony, the shoulders of a fierce old warrior, not like an old woman's at all.

She patted my knee. "We'd best go back and join the others," she said, her brisk, no-nonsense self again, and I realized our meeting had just been adjourned. Before she escaped, though, I hugged her one more time. "Thanks again for remembering my ribbon, Nana," I said. She smiled, and I thought her eyes looked shiny, like maybe there were tears in them. But she was like me. She clamped her jaw, and didn't shed a single one.

There was no limit to the number of hot dogs those turkeys Derek and Jason could eat. Skipper watched them pig out as if they were Greek gods—which they weren't, they were still a pair of prune pits—but everyone needs heroes, and for the moment Derek and Jason were his.

For a while after we ate everyone played Trivial Pursuit under the dim light of the Chinese lanterns, then just before the ice cream was ready to be served, Vinnie invited me to walk around the block with him.

"Remember the walks we used to have after supper?" he asked as we started up the street. I was surprised he'd mention such a thing. When we passed Mr. Byerly's yard, Prince couldn't understand why he wasn't invited to come along.

"What I remember is, you never wanted to hold hands," I reminded Vinnie. That's when I almost fainted, because he reached over and took mine. We laced our fingers together and started up the other side of the block.

"It seemed embarrassing at the time," my brother admitted with a grin. "I was in my superhero phase then. Superheroes don't hold hands."

"So how is it, living with Nana and Papa?" I hoped Vinnie's answer would explain to me what had gone on upstairs in my room.

"Different people have different ways of coping," he said, sounding like some sort of expert. I didn't see how he could be; I never figured Vinnie to be much of a deep thinker. "But it's been hard for them," he said. "I mean, I'm not Dad. Having me live with them— well, Glennie, it's not like they thought it would be. I couldn't just step in and actually *be* the person Dad was, which would give them a chance to turn back the clock and start all over again from the beginning. I think they've finally admitted I'm someone else. I'm just, well, just me. I can only be Vinnie, not anybody else."

I studied my brother's new beard. "I bet *that* went over like a lead balloon."

He grinned. "Nana and I had a talk about it, for sure," he confessed. "You know our Nana—she has a picture in her head of what's right and what's wrong." Suddenly I was glad I hadn't invited Cooper to the picnic, as I'd briefly thought of doing. Even though she'd changed a little, there was no way a guy like him would fit Nana's what's-right list.

When we got back for ice cream, I sat between my mother and Wanda at one of the folding tables. "You and Wanda and Skipper really seem to be quite a cozy little family," my mother said, smiling in her vague, visitor-from-outer-space way.

"For a substitute family, they've been really great," I whispered when Wanda turned aside to talk to Aunt Helen and I was sure she couldn't hear me. "Of course, when we all get down to Albuquerque. . . ."

"That might not happen very soon," my mother murmured, and looked off across Wanda's next-door neighbor's yard.

"Oh, not till you feel better," I agreed. "But as soon as you do . . ."

All she said was, "Ummm," the way people do when they don't want to tell you something you're not ready to hear. She smoothed her hair behind her ears, and I noticed the place where her ring used to be was still pale and empty.

When the picnic was over, my mother was the first to leave because she had to catch the evening bus back to Fair Haven. I figured it would be a good time to return her vanilla-colored sweater, so I did.

"Oh, Glennis, how thoughtful of you to have taken such good care of it," she said, caressing it and giving me a little child's sweet, surprised smile. Vinnie drove her down to the station in my grandparents' car, and I wondered what they said to each other, if she told him anything about that pale band on her finger, or about Albuquerque and luminarias.

The prune pits left next. Uncle Roger had to carry the twins out to his van, though; they were sticky and damp and asleep on their feet. I kissed each of them good-bye, but they were too zonked to kiss me back. Then Robert and Ramona linked arms with their precious pear and they left, too. Louise gave me a cuddly good-bye hug.

"Come and stay with me some weekend after school's out," she said. I noticed the invitation was for a defined length of time. I wasn't being invited to spend the whole summer, much less the rest of my life.

My grandparents were the last to go. My grandmother took both of Wanda's hands in her own, and trained on her the level look of someone about to bestow an award. "What you did today was thoughtful and lovely, Wanda," she said, words that turned my aunt pink with pleasure and made her giggle. We said good-bye at the curb, then Vinnie drove down the street, turned the corner at Byerly's (Prince barked a final farewell), and they were gone.

Then it was just the three of us again. Wanda, Skipper, me.

Wanda flopped on the couch with a happy sigh. "I hate to tell you this, Glen, for fear it might make you conceited, but putting on a picnic was just about the best idea you ever had. Did you notice even old Mrs. R. seemed pleased?"

Skipper was almost too pooped to speak. "It was . . . the best day . . . I ever had," he croaked finally. "Next year . . . let's do it . . . all over again."

"It'll be Roger's turn next time," Wanda said. "We agreed to take turns from now on. In a way, that'll be even more fun. The year after that, Robert and Ramona want to do it. And Roger said he'll make us a copy of the video he made today so we can watch ourselves having a good time."

I left the two of them in front of the TV while I went out to the backyard to pick up some crumpled paper napkins and a couple of cups that had rolled into a corner next to Skipper's rusty old swing-set. A sparrow sat on the edge of the window box, looking pleased by the new flowers. It was that lavender time of evening when nothing much seems to be going on in the world, when everyone's gone indoors and little kids are getting ready for bed while parents settle down in front of the tube.

Except something major happened to me. Right then, right while I was standing there in Wanda's backyard in Burnsville, Ohio. Just as I heard Mr. Byerly call for Prince to come into the house. At the precise moment the sparrow flew away from the window box and vanished into the twilit dark.

All of a sudden, *I knew.*

Knew everyone had a different life now. Vinnie, Louise, the twins. Mom. Me. Everyone. The old Humpty Dumpty life I came to Burnsville to glue back together wasn't ever going to get fixed up. I might as well forget about finding a yellow brick road leading back home. That could only happen in the movies to a girl from Kansas named Dorothy who never had to give up her dog.

So, for a few minutes, I just stood there alone in Wanda's backyard, and cried in the quiet lavender dark.

Not the gasping, choking, terrible crying a person does when their favorite pooch goes off to live with someone else. It was the soft kind that washes your heart and leaves you clean and drained and empty. The way you cry when you finally admit to yourself that your old life is over. For keeps.

🌺 *Chapter Fourteen*

I had rehearsed my speech so often in front of the cracked mirror in Wanda's upstairs bathroom, I knew it almost by heart. Not to mention that I'd given it to Skipper so many times. I swear he knew it better than I did, and if I skipped anything he always reminded me what I'd left out.

"The swan is one of the loveliest birds in all the world, with its graceful neck curved in the shape of an S, with its sleek feathers that are as white as snow. No city park would be complete without a pond that has swans floating on it." I thought of the swans on the Mumfords' pond, but now the ones in Burnsville seemed to matter more.

"Swans have played an important part in legends and fairy tales. A ballet called *Swan Lake* was written about a dying swan, and artists have painted pictures of these birds since ancient times." Actually, I was surprised how much I'd learned about them. First from Cooper, then from all the books I'd read.

"But not all swans are white," I pointed out, "and one species of swan is mute. That doesn't mean it can't make any sound at all, though. The noise it's able to make is a soft, chirring sound, sort of like one a mother raccoon makes to her kits."

In my speech, I intended that my classmates would learn more about swans than they'd ever wanted to know. Mrs. McCarthy would be so impressed, I'd get an *A* for sure—not that *A*'s were such a big deal to me anymore.

Only three speeches were given each day, to make sure none of us got too bored. Grady had just finished his speech, which was about animal shelters, how much it cost to run them, how folks who work there take care of other creatures besides dogs and cats—badgers, raccoons, and snakes, for example. Mary had given hers first, about a vacation she took to Alaska, and she showed a picture of herself standing on the Matanuska Glacier, which she said melts a little bit every year.

When it was my turn, I steadied my hands after I dried them off on the knees of my jeans. It made me nervous to watch a speaker whose paper fluttered like a sail in a high wind. The class looked at me expectantly. I looked back at them.

Then I gave a speech I'd never practiced. Not once. A speech I didn't know I knew, one that surprised me even more than it did my audience.

"Every Saturday morning for the first three months after I moved here to Burnsville, I caught the eight A.M. bus on the corner a half a block from my aunt Wanda's house over on Owen Street. You know, down there by the railroad tracks."

Glennis Reilly, what are you doing?

"I put a dollar's worth of tokens in the coin box,

125

then ate an apple as I rode two miles out to the Federal Detention Center on the edge of town. You all know where it is. Some of you probably have moms or dads who work there. Going out to the FDC every Saturday was the main reason I usually couldn't do things regular kids do. Like go to sleepovers on Friday nights and stuff like that, because I always had to get up so early the next day."

Mary's eyes got round. LuAnn stared at me, astonished. Grady's mouth was a perfect *O* of amazement. Mrs. McCarthy blanched, and raised her fingers to her throat. Nobody squirmed. No one fidgeted. If anyone had dropped a pin, the noise in Room 114 would have sounded like a cannon going off.

"Every Saturday morning for three months, I went out to the prison to see my father."

Glennis Reilly, this is the end of Life as You Knew It.

"My dad didn't murder anyone. He didn't steal secrets from the government or sell drugs or kidnap anybody and hold them for a million dollars' ransom."

Glennis Reilly, even if you live to be a hundred, no one will ever ask you to a sleepover again.

"My dad's what newspapers and TV commentators call a white-collar criminal. He was sentenced to prison for ten years for committing savings and loan fraud. That means he misused the money people had invested in his company. He'll have to serve at least three years of his time before he's eligible for his first parole hearing. When that happens, I'll be almost sixteen years old."

Mrs. McCarthy hugged herself as if the room had suddenly gotten drafty, and watched me even more breathlessly than the rest of the class did.

"My father's a prisoner," I said, "and I'm a prisoner's daughter.'' No one in the room moved. If I didn't get an *A* for the content of my speech, I sure ought to get one for keeping everyone glued to their seats.

"After my dad went to prison, some awful things happened to my family. My mom had a nervous breakdown. That means a person just can't cope anymore. My mother sort of gave up, you know? She didn't even care if she combed her hair or brushed her teeth, and had to go to a treatment center called Fair Haven.'' I told them about Vinnie and Louise and the twins. It was hard to put all of it into words, and my voice got quivery, but one part made me get really choky.

"We had to give our dog away, too. We got Rags the year I was seven. On Christmas Eve. He came in a cardboard box, and had a red bow tied around his neck. He was a gold-and-white collie, and for the first week he slept in that box right next to my bed because he was so little and scared of being all by himself. My dad wrapped an old alarm clock up in a towel and put it in beside Rags. He said the ticking of the clock would remind Rags of the sound of his mother's heartbeat. It worked, too, so if any of you ever get a puppy for Christmas, be sure you get an alarm clock, too.''

You'd have thought for sure I was one of Skipper's favorite TV shows. Every eyeball was fastened on me by invisible wires, as if I were the best Road Runner cartoon ever cranked out.

I cleared my throat. My speech was off-the-cuff; since I hadn't planned to give it, I hadn't rehearsed a word of it. Suddenly I realized I'd come to a fork in the road, and didn't exactly know which direction to turn.

"The reason I decided to make a speech about why I'm living here in Burnsville with my aunt Wanda and my cousin Skipper is because . . . because . . .''

Because why?

"Because I found out not all prisons are made out of stone, and spiders aren't the only ones who can weave webs," I said. "A person can build a prison out of anything. Like . . . like . . ."

Like what?

"Like you can build one out of words," I said. "By using words to pretend other people aren't who they really are. By pretending you're somebody you're not. That you'll never be again."

My grandmother knew all about that now, too. I glanced at Mrs. McCarthy. I could tell she was remembering my journal, all that stuff about my skinny, nervous sister named Laura, my mother who was a famous model in New York, and my dad who was a photographer for *National Geographic*. She smiled at me, and nodded her head slightly.

"In the beginning, see, I didn't want to believe my dad was guilty. I figured there was this humongous mistake that a new trial would fix. I wanted to believe we could get our old life back. To me, my dad was the greatest person in the world. I mean, he was the one who had the idea about putting an alarm clock in Rags's box, right? And you know something? In a way, maybe he *was* a great dad. Maybe he still is."

I was startled to hear myself admit that. What if it was true?

"Because you know what my dad did a few weeks ago? He opened a door for me that I couldn't open by myself. He told me he was guilty. He got caught in a web that he wove himself. He said there's a saying out there at the prison: You do the crime, you do the time. So now he has to pay for what he did. Sometimes, people make prisons out of the things they wish were true, but my dad decided not to let me do that. So, anyway. Now you know why I came to Burnsville to live.''

I walked back to my seat and sat down. Everyone let their breath out. Slowly. Adam Brusky looked at me in a way that let me know he'd never in a million trillion years make any tennis-Glennis cracks to me.

"Whew," Grady said under his breath. "Some speech." Everyone laughed. It was weird; it was the nicest sound I'd heard since I left Kenwood. I'd finally walked all the way up the stairs from that place deep inside. Light seemed to shine into the dark corners down there. All the corners except one. Except where I kept my grudge against my dad locked up in a box that didn't have a key.

After school, before Wanda got home and while Skipper was practicing some of his wrestling exercises on the mattress he dragged off his bed and moved into the living room, I had a chance to make the phone call I'd wanted to make ever since I got on the bus with two suitcases and my backpack to come to live in Burnsville.

"Mrs. Mumford?" I said when she answered the phone. The lump in my throat made it hard to talk. "This is Glennis Reilly. Do you remember me? What I was wondering, well, how's Rags doing?"

"Why, Glennis, of course I remember you! It's really nice to hear from you, dear." She paused for a moment, as if she was so surprised that she didn't know what to say next. I suppose she hadn't expected to hear from any of the Reillys ever again, like they'd fallen off the edge of the world or something.

"Rags is just fine, Glennis. Oh, there were a few days at the beginning when he didn't have much appetite, and it seemed as if he spent an awful lot of time just looking down the road, waiting for one of you Reilly kids to come back and rescue him. Of course, we had to keep him on a tether until he got over his homesickeness. You know how it is with pets that have lived such a long time with just one family.''

I wanted to tell her it wasn't that much different with people. They look down roads and get lonesome and wait to be rescued, too.

''But the kids brought him out of his doldrums,'' she went on. ''Nancy groomed him by the hour, said he was more fun to brush than a Barbie. And Toby played chase-the-ball with him in the yard until I thought they'd wear each other out.''

Listening to her, I felt so funny. Glad and sad at the same time. Glad that Rags had a good home now, that he was happy and was getting brushed and played with and loved, but sad it wasn't me who was doing the brushing and playing and loving.

''Your house on Stone Barn Road has a new family in it now,'' Mrs. Mumford told me. ''Nice people, with three little kids, all girls. One of them has your old room, Glennis, the one at the back of the house.''

A little girl would grow up in my old room. She'd sit on the seat under the big window that once had been mine. Surrounded by her family, she'd feel safe and happy, like I had once. Maybe they'd all walk up Stone Barn Road after supper and hold hands. When Mrs. Mumford hung up, I sat on the couch for a while and watched Skipper do his stretching exercises. I should have felt terrible. In a weird way, though, the bruised pigeon under my ribs felt almost like my old heart.

Chapter Fifteen

This time, I didn't look straight ahead and pretend not to see any of the other passengers when I got on the bus. Knowing what I was going to do when I got to the FDC made me feel different. I'd found the key to that box where I kept my grudge against John Reilly. Today, I'd use it.

I looked at everyone as I walked down the aisle toward the back. When I got to Mrs. Cinnamon Buns, she glanced up, smiled, and patted the seat next to her. "Why, it's lovely to see you again, dear. We've all missed you."

I could see Cooper wasn't on the bus, so I sat down. "This week, the fellows out at the FDC asked for chocolate chip cookies with extra chips," Mrs. Buns said as soon as I got settled.

"The fellows?" I echoed. It sounded as if she'd decided to bake for other guys besides her son. Then I realized I really believed the story I'd made up about her having a son who'd gone off to college to be a lawyer and messed up his whole life by dealing drugs.

"Yes, indeed. I've been doing this ever since I retired from my job at the post office." She smiled at me as if we'd known each other for a long time. "I'm a member of a volunteer group, you know. We call ourselves The Friends of Prisoners." She tapped the white box on her knees. "Would you like one before we arrive?" she asked. I took a cookie when she lifted the lid. She must've baked first thing this morning, because they were still warm and soft in the middle.

"My name's Edith Taylor," Mrs. Cinnamon Buns said. It was had to think of her as Edith Taylor, when to me she'd always been a lady named Cinnamon Buns. When we got to the FDC, I stepped aside in the aisle so she could get off first, which meant I accidentally bumped into the Movie Star.

"Oops, sorry," I mumbled.

"Oh, it's my fault, hon," she apologized right back. "I'm just not quite with it this morning." She took off her dark glasses, and I saw that her eyes were blue and tired. "I was up late last night with Jackie. He's got the flu, the upchucky kind, and he feels just awful. You know how cranky little kids can be when they don't feel good."

In my story, she didn't have any little kids. She was waiting for a deal in Hollywood. "He misses his daddy, you know, and now that he's sick, he can't understand why Daddy can't come to cheer him up. When you're only four, you don't know about prisons and doing time and all that." She talked to me as if she was sure I understood the situation perfectly. "Next year, when he's a little older, maybe I'll bring him out for a visit. It'll mean a lot to both Jackie and his daddy."

Inside, Dad was sitting in a corner at a card table, and had just laid out a game of solitaire. I wondered if he'd come to the waiting room all those Saturdays that I'd never shown up, thinking maybe, just maybe, I'd come along sooner or later. He got up quickly when he saw me, and hugged me as if he'd really missed me. His backbone didn't seem as knobby as before, and there weren't any dark circles under his eyes.

"I'm glad you took my advice about making a new life, Bunny," he whispered against my forehead. "Just the same, I have to admit I was beginning to enjoy your visits once a week!"

The first thing I wanted to do was apologize about the invitation I'd him. But he held a finger to my lips and said, "Shush, Glennis. You don't have to explain. I understand what you were trying to tell me." Then he wanted to know how the picnic went and how everyone looked. He studied his knuckles a moment before he asked about my mother.

"I think she'll be all right," I said. "Not real soon, but Wanda says she's stronger than I give her credit for." Then I told him about my speech. Also about my first sleepover at Mary's. He put his cards aside, and held my hands while we talked. When I looked into his eyes, they didn't seem like dark wells anymore. They were just brown eyes. A little sad. A little regretful, like my own, but without any shadows behind them.

"Dad, I want you to know I forgive you," I said. The words came out fast, because I wanted to get them said before he could stop me. His eyes got shiny, like Nana's when she sat on the edge of the bed in my room. He gave me an extra hug and kissed the top of my head.

"I'll see you in two weeks," I said when visiting time was over. This time, I didn't make any vows about staying in Burnsville till he got out. Instead, I explained that on some Saturdays I'd be busy with Mary and Kara-lyn and wouldn't be able to make it to the FDC. I could tell that made him almost as happy as going to my school concerts once did.

As I walked out to the bus, I realized the Godfather was walking only one step behind me. He'd traded his beautiful fawn-colored coat for a tan raincoat, and I saw a crisp white collar circling his neck.

"Good morning, F-F-Father," I stammered.

"Reverend, as in the Episcopal kind," he corrected with a smile. "I heard Miss Taylor welcome you back, young lady. I'll second the motion." His smile was easy and comfortable, and he seemed to know that I was curious. "I come here every Saturday to intervene for men who need the sort of help I can offer," he said. "It's good for me, and good for them."

How wrong I'd been about everything! About Edith Taylor, the Movie Star, my dad, my family. Myself. All because I made up stories instead of letting people be who they really were.

The Reverend boarded the bus, but I waved good-bye to the grandpa driver and told him I was going to walk back to town. It was so warm, I took off my windbreaker and tied the arms around my waist.

I could see Cooper from quite far away. He must have finished up early, and was sitting on a bench where he could keep an eye on the bike path. My heart gave a little *thonk* when I realized maybe he was watching for me. I waved, and he waved back

When I got close, he smiled, and I wished Nana had had a chance to meet a person with taupe-colored eyes. "I was wondering if I'd see you before I left," he said. "I've got something for you." He reached into his pocket and took out a piece of paper folded into fourths.

The poem was called *She's Different Now.*

The first time I saw her on the bus
She was carrying an apple,
And never looked at anyone—
Especially me.
It was March, still so cold
It seemed as if spring would never come.
But the ice has melted, the swans have cygnets
   now,
And I think her heart is free.

"Thanks," I said. Now, if I grew up to be a girl who never got married because nobody asked her, not even Adam Brusky, I'd still have a poem that some boy had written for me. I could read it when I got old, when I had to fill my spare time baby-sitting for all the kids Louise and Whit Anderson would have.

"So what did you mean, before you leave?" I asked.

"Next week I'll be all done with my community service," Cooper said. "Then I'm gonna be discharged from PORT."

"Then what?"

"I think I'll go out to Wyoming and stay with my grandparents." Wyoming seemed as far away as New Mexico, and sounded just as empty and full of sky. "Maybe I can get a job. Or go to school. Out there, no one will know anything about me. Means I can sorta start over." He gave me a sly glance. "Who knows, maybe I'll be a cowboy." If he was going to be gone so soon, it meant if I intended to tell him anything, I'd better do it quick.

"I'm glad you still had some community service to do when I came to Burnsville," I told him. "So that I could get to know you." How else would I have found out about prisons that aren't made out of stones?

We sat for a while and didn't say anything. "Isn't it funny? I mean, what happens?" I said. It was basically the same question my grandmother had put to me. "Once, I thought life was a happily-ever-after kind of thing. Like it is on sitcoms. I found out it wasn't, at least not the way I thought."

We walked slowly back to town, the empty pail bonking against his knee first, mine next. We stopped where I had to turn up Owen Street, and Cooper stuck out his hand. "Keep the faith, Glennis," he said. I told him I would, as soon as I figured out for sure what it was. "I've got your address," he added, "so maybe I'll send you a postcard when I get out there to Wyoming."

"Thanks for the poem," I said. Then I did something totally stupid. Something I'd never done in my life. More unexpected even than the speech I gave about my dad. A thing my sister Louise, who was a hugger, might have understood.

I kissed Cooper Davis on the cheek.

Right there in broad daylight on the corner of Owen Street and Logan Avenue. His face was warm against mine; he tasted salty, and his hair smelled of barbecue smoke from the Burger Bonanza. I turned and ran up the street, and when I got to Wanda's house I turned around to see if he was still there, if he would wave back at me. But he was gone, so I said into the air, hoping the words would grow wings, would fly down the street after him, might perch on the rim of his ear: "Hey, Cooper. Don't forget about that postcard. And you keep the faith, too."

*   *   *

After Wanda got home from work, she decided to make lasagna for supper. She said she had a special recipe. "Is it one from scratch?" Skipper wanted to know, and looked suspiciously at the section of the cupboard that used to hold boxes of macaroni and cheese. Wanda smiled, and stirred his hair with her fingers. I made tomato and cucumber salad while Skipper set the table. He even put out some salad forks, which all had crooked tines.

"Oh, hon, don't fuss with those beat-up old things," Wanda said, but he did anyway. "It makes the table look fancy," he said. "Even if it's only for us."

Only for us. The words made Skipper smile. He hooked his hands behind his back and studied the table. "It's like one I saw over at Buster's house." He was doing even better on Saturday mornings since he'd started practicing his wrestling moves with Buster. "You know, like when people are going to have company for supper. We're getting to be more and more like other people, Momma, now that we got Glennis."

Skipper and Wanda had me. I had them. I'd never live in a white house on a hill again. Maybe not in a brown adobe one in Albuquerque, either. Once, to realize such things would've broken my heart all over again, as if somebody had trampled Humpty Dumpty's poor cracked body till it was fine as dust.

"Hey, Skipper," I said, "after supper, you want to go down to the corner and get Mr. Byerly's dog? We could walk Prince up to the playground and back, okay?" I wondered if, just by accident, Adam Brusky would be there, just hanging out.

We sat down, and Skipper said grace. He'd learned it in Sunday school, which he'd just started going to.

He wanted us all to hold hands, so we did. His voice was clear and firm. "For health and food, for love and friends, for everything Thy goodness sends, amen."

We dug into the lasagna, and Skipper declared it was even better than Buster's mom made. I passed the salad around, while my mind sort of wandered. Out in the living room, I heard Lewis begin to sing one of his favorite songs. It only had three notes in it, but he sang them so deliriously that I felt the leftover ache under my breastbone soften. After a little while, I couldn't feel it at all. Lewis didn't know it, but to me his song sounded like it had something to do with forgiveness.

"I'll do the dishes tonight," Wanda told us. "You guys go on up to the playground if you want. Just get home before dark, okay?" Outside, I hooked pinky fingers with Skipper, and we started up the street. Prince barked as soon as he saw us coming, and began to leap around his yard as if he could hardly wait for us to get there. Before was gone forever; this was after. Somehow, it was going to be all right.